### STAMPEDE
Thundering buffalo turned about in a single, heaving mass, running full out and goring to death any horse that stood in the way.

### SHIPWRECKED
Starving, barefoot, a slave in a land of strangers, the ragged man stubbornly walked for home — half a continent away.

### DEATH AT SEA
The creaking ship's desperate crew weakly sailed north, through dark waves and arctic cold. Then, suddenly, they were gone . . .

### DEVILS, TALKING SNAKES, AND LUMINOUS CITIES OF GOLD
The greedy, the bold, and the curious — they all gambled on what wealth and wonders they might find just over the mysterious horizons.

## WHEN THE WILD WEST WAS THE WILD, WILD NORTH, PALE-FACED ADVENTURERS ROAMED UP FROM MEXICO

# INTO THE UNKNOWN
The language was Spanish, and these explorers from far away answered to the king's viceroy, but the rush, the thrill that they knew also would be the same centuries later for the mountain men and American pioneers pushing west. Going where no non-Indian had gone before, these questing men — and women — struggled and searched in a raw, new world, enticed by a lure sometimes stronger than even gold — the power of a wildly beautiful, unknown country.

Read other books in the
WILD WEST COLLECTION,
fast-paced, real-life stories of when the Old West was still young and rowdy, where anything could happen — and too often did.

### DAYS OF DESTINY
### MANHUNTS & MASSACRES
### THEY LEFT THEIR MARK
### THE LAW OF THE GUN
### TOMBSTONE CHRONICLES
### STALWART WOMEN

Turn to the back of this book to read more about them.

Design: MARY WINKELMAN VELGOS
Copy Editor: EVELYN HOWELL
Research: JEB STUART ROSEBROOK
Production: ELLEN STRAINE
Photographic enhancement: VICKY SNOW
Front cover art: Computer-generated illustration by VICKY SNOW
based on photographs by SUSAN HAZEN-HAMMOND
Tooled leather design on covers: KEVIN KIBSEY AND RONDA JOHNSON-FREEMAN
Book Editor: BOB ALBANO

Prepared by the Book Division of *Arizona Highways*® magazine, a monthly
publication of the Arizona Department of Transportation.

Publisher — Nina M. La France
Managing Editor — Bob Albano
Associate Editor — Evelyn Howell
Art Director — Mary Winkelman Velgos
Production Director — Cindy Mackey

Printed in the United States
Library of Congress Catalog Number 99-62101
ISBN 0-916179-84-2

# INTO THE UNKNOWN

## Adventure on the
## Spanish Colonial Frontier

by SUSAN HAZEN-HAMMOND

# ACKNOWLEDGMENTS

Scholars whose work has most strongly influenced mine include David J. Weber, Donald C. Cutter, Oakah L. Jones, Marc Simmons, Warren L. Cook, Stan Hordes, George P. Hammond, Agapito Rey, Herbert Eugene Bolton, Charles Wilson Hackett, and France V. Scholes. Stan Hordes offered his support and encouragement at every step. José Antonio Esquibel honored and assisted me by reading the manuscript and making numerous excellent suggestions.

Librarians Laura Holt, Ingrid Vollnhofer, Guadalupe Martinez, Norma McCallan, Valerie Brooker, Joanne Werger, and many others have helped me in a thousand different ways. Without them, I would never have completed this book.

On a personal level, William and Beth Hammond, Eduardo Fuss, Susan Arritt, Karl and Angela Storch, Schia Muterperl, Iska Sargent, Mary Cable, Ken Macrorie, Judy Roberts, Elena and Flavio Garcia, Bill and Barbara Murphy, Kurt and Dianna Duerre, and, above all, Kenneth Duerre and Paul Golding provided a warm, nurturing environment for me while I worked on this book.

My deepest thanks to each of you.

Susan Hazen-Hammond was born in the West and has lived in six western states: Arizona, California, Montana, Nevada, New Mexico, and Washington.

She likes to say that she started reading the journals and reports of the Spanish colonial era one day in 1980 and didn't look up again for 20 years, but we think that's just her own brand of magical realism (see the chapter entitled Magical Realism on the Frontier). What is provable is that she accepted her first assignment from *Arizona Highways* in 1982 and wrote an article about Antonio de Espejo. She's been writing about the Spanish colonial era ever since.

Hazen-Hammond speaks, reads, and writes Spanish and has traveled widely in the Spanish-speaking world. Her writings appear throughout Latin America in the popular Spanish magazine, *Selecciones*, and one of her articles earned the *Primer Premio Nacional de Periodismo* (National First Prize in Journalism) in Mexico in 1995. Her poetry in Spanish appears in the quarterly, *La Herencia del Norte*.

Hazen-Hammond is the author of eight other books, including two history books: *Timelines of Native American History* (1997), which was designated an alternate selection by the Quality Paperback Book Club, and the regionally popular *Short History of Santa Fe* (1988). Her other books include *Spider Woman's Web: Traditional Native American Tales about Women's Power* (1999) and *Thunder Bear and Ko: The Buffalo Nation and Nambe Pueblo* (1999). Her book

*Chile Pepper Fever: Mine's Hotter than Yours* received the Benjamin Franklin award in 1994.

Hazen-Hammond is also a photographer. In 1998, one of her photographs was reproduced on a U.S. postage stamp commemorating 400 years of Spanish settlement in the Southwest (see the Epilogue).

Readers who'd like a complete list of works that Hazen-Hammond consulted for this book or an annotated copy of her manuscript may contact the author at P.O. Box 8400, Santa Fe, New Mexico 87504-8400. "If you have time to read just one more book," she says, "choose David Weber's brilliant volume, *The Spanish Frontier in North America*. Weber is not only an extraordinary historian, but also a gifted writer."

# When the Wild West Was the Wild North

O NE AFTERNOON 20 YEARS AGO, SOON AFTER I MOVED FROM Washington state to New Mexico, I came across Diego Pérez de Luxán's journal of the Espejo expedition in 1582-83 into what is now Arizona, New Mexico, and Texas. I started reading and couldn't stop, as Pérez de Luxán's simple, powerful sentences re-created the world the explorers found themselves in.

Early in February 1583, Pérez de Luxán wrote of the Pueblo Indians, "They are clean and tidy, and do not smell." At Cochiti Pueblo, he wrote, "They gave us corn, tortillas, turkeys, and pinole. We bartered sleigh bells and small iron articles for very fine buffalo hides." Approaching Zuni on March 10: "We slept in the woods because it snowed so much that we were unable to proceed. We went to bed without water, and this day drank snow water melted in pots and pans."

For the first time, history became more than words in a book for me as I read what the explorers thought, felt, saw, tasted, heard, smelled, and did — in the very region I myself was beginning to love.

Today, I pick up the first non-fiction classic of the West, Alvar Núñez Cabeza de Vaca's first-person *Adventures in the Unknown Interior of America*, and read the words, "They cast away their daughters at birth; the dogs eat them." I am still hooked, as I reread the shipwrecked sailor's account of the brutal war zone that existed among the Indians of Texas when Europeans arrived.

Almost 500 years have passed since Spanish explorer Alonso Alvarez de Pineda and his fellow sailors set foot on the beaches of Texas in 1519, becoming the first known

Europeans in what is now the American West. Ever since then, this vast, mythic, extravagant expanse of land has seduced, bewitched, frightened, battered, and fascinated succeeding generations of non-Indians who attempt to make it their own.

Early on, the whole of what now is the American West was known as Nuevo México, with a mysterious island called California somewhere out in the "South Sea" — the Pacific As late as 1763, even writers in England asserted that New Mexico — Nuevo México — extended "a great way towards the North Pole."

In one sense, that was true. On the basis of explorations that ranged from Alaska to Texas and from California to the Dakotas, Spain claimed it all, right up to the North Pole. Then Spain lost it all, from the North Pole to the South. In North America, the Spanish colonial era lasted until 1821, when New Spain (Mexico) gained independence from Spain, and Spain's greatly diminished holdings in the north became part of Mexico.

Throughout the Spanish colonial era, what we now think of as the American West remained frontier. The accent was Spanish, the state religion Roman Catholic, the Inquisition a fact of life. The non-Indians who lived and traveled here considered this the Wild North instead of the Wild West. The Indians were many, and the Spanish colonists few. Otherwise, though, long before the United States came into existence, many of the elements we associate with the Wild West already were present.

Pioneers wrestled with the land and themselves. They fought off Apaches. They didn't pretend to be saints; they gambled, swore, shot their friends, and engaged in tempestuous affairs. Sometimes they created — or lived in — unbelievable mayhem. And they came from all over. Five Portuguese, two Italians, a Frenchman, a Scotsman, and a German accompanied the various parties in don Francisco Vázquez de Coronado's expedition in 1540-42.

The very first travelers set the pattern of rugged individualism, raw courage, inventiveness, and the ability to survive seemingly impossible circumstances that have characterized the West ever since. Some people couldn't wait to get here. Others couldn't leave fast enough. But through the centuries, those who reached the northern frontier of New Spain shared this bond: They lived and died, lured — and sometimes driven — by the power and appeal of the unknown.

The stories included here all relate to this theme. The Wild North presented one kind of Great Unknown for Alvar Núñez Cabeza de Vaca, the West's first, magnificent, archetypal hero, when he washed ashore on a Texas beach in 1528. It presented another for the early settlers, who found life in the Wild North far different than they had imagined. In 1807, a still different Great Unknown faced Governor Joaquín del Real Alencaster, when Mongo Meri Paike, the American explorer Zebulon Montgomery Pike, arrived unwanted and illegally on the northern frontier of New Spain.

By then, Spanish colonial officials suspected that Americans would overrun the Wild North. They saw these unkempt newcomers as greedy, bloodthirsty, and driven by a lust for gold.

The irony is that for centuries English-speaking peoples and other non-Spanish Europeans have seen Spain and all of the Spanish colonial era through the dark veil of *la leyenda negra*, the Black Legend that said that anything Spanish was bad, evil, corrupt. It wasn't true, of course. Or rather it was, but only to the degree that all of us, in all times and places, carry within us some element of evil.

Perhaps to make peace with the dark side of the Spanish colonial era, we should remember that the past truly is a foreign country. We must always be cautious in judging it or imagining we understand it.

So many years and generations have passed that many documents have vanished, or been destroyed, used for such unbelievable purposes as lighting cigars, or wrapping slabs of fresh meat. Fortunately, Spanish explorers and officials wrote constantly. For New Spain alone, 1,500 volumes of documents survive just from the workings of the Inquisition, the infamous tribunal that tread on human rights as it sought to stamp out heresy and sedition.

The stories presented in *Into the Unknown* are taken from the accounts of the original travelers and adventurers. Unbelievable but true, these tales of adventure, hardship, and daring explore a long-neglected chapter of the Wild West.

## A NOTE ON WEIGHTS, MEASURES, PLACES, AND TRIBES

When Spanish explorers and colonists measured distances, weights, and lengths, they thought in terms of *leguas* (leagues), *fanegas*, *varas*, and similar units. These varied in quantity from era to era, place to place, even substance to substance. A *fanega* of corn equaled about 100 present-day pounds; a *fanega* of wheat only 80. In general, I have used modern terms: miles, pounds, and yards, except occasionally for historical flavor.

Scholars disagree vigorously about many details of the route of virtually every single explorer in the Spanish colonial era. When I tentatively suggest present-day landmarks, or the present-day names of Indian tribes, I am simply providing the reader with a point of reference.

Occasionally, where custom dictates, I have kept the Anglicized version of Spanish names. For instance, I refer to Francisco Vázquez de Coronado as Coronado, rather than as Vázquez de Coronado, or simply Vázquez.

# CHAPTER ONE

# Alvar Núñez Cabeza de Vaca

## Shipwreck Survivor Lives Naked and Alone

*Lightning, cold, and hunger tormented
Alvar Núñez Cabeza de Vaca. Indians
enslaved him. Assassins tried to kill him.
His only friend abandoned him. But his wits,
his faith, and his dreams kept the
Wild West's first great hero alive.*

———⟐———

COLD WINDS WERE BLOWING ACROSS THE PLAINS AND HILLS of south Texas. People stuffed their bellies with the last prickly pear fruits before winter hunger set in. When a man from the Susolas tribe sickened and fell unconscious, his relatives sent for a traveling medicine man who was visiting a nearby tribe.

But before the medicine man arrived, the patient's pulse ceased. His eyes rolled back in their sockets. His distraught relatives wailed as they covered him with a mat and prepared to burn his house.

When the medicine man arrived, he pulled back the mat and blew his breath into the face of the corpse. He blessed the deceased, made movements with his hands, and prayed in a language none of the villagers understood.

Again and again the medicine man repeated this ritual. In gratitude, the family presented him with the dead man's bow and a basket of pounded prickly pears.

The medicine man moved on to treat some ill villagers

who had fallen into a stupor. Their grateful relatives loaded him with cactus fruits, too.

That evening, villagers appeared at the medicine man's hut. "The dead man has come to life," they said. "You are truly a Child of the Sun."

Alvar Núñez Cabeza de Vaca neither looked nor felt like a child of the sun. In the past seven years, he had known so much hunger that he resembled a skeleton covered with skin. He walked naked, with not even coverings to protect his feet. Deep cuts gashed his arms. Sores covered his chest and shoulders. And he knew how vulnerable he was. He had no training as a healer. His only aids were his ability to watch and mimic others, the trust of the people who came to him, and his devout faith in God.

If the sick he treated died too often, or if he himself fell ill, these people would enslave him or plot to murder him, as others had before. Even if he could escape murder, slavery, starvation, and the elements, there was no guaranteeing he would achieve his dream of reuniting with Spanish colonists and soldiers.

The bearded castaway and former soldier didn't even know where his people were. He believed he would find them farther south, but he also had heard reports that the Spaniards lived to the north.

With these thoughts and concerns on his mind, Cabeza de Vaca whispered prayers of gratitude and supplication. It was 1534 — six years after he and 90 other survivors from the disastrous Narváez expedition to Florida had washed ashore on their homemade barges near present-day Galveston, Texas. For most of that time, he had lived among the Indians.

During the first year, he labored as a slave of the Capoques, along the coast. With bleeding fingers, he dug underwater roots, a task normally reserved for women. Even the wealthiest among his captors lived in simple homes made of woven mats and slept on floors of crushed oyster shells.

About February 1530, he escaped and found himself free

to wander and live as he pleased. He could have set out at once for Mexico, but he still didn't know whether to travel north or south, and he had an even bigger reason for staying. He knew of only one castaway who had survived, Lope de Oviedo. The man was living alone among the Indians along the coast. As badly as Cabeza de Vaca wanted to go, he didn't want to leave Oviedo behind.

Whenever he could, Cabeza de Vaca visited Oviedo on the coastal island where he lived and begged him to leave. Each time Oviedo's answer was the same: "Let's go next year. I'm not ready to leave now."

While he waited, Cabeza de Vaca supported himself by working as an itinerant trader.

To inland tribes he brought seashells, including conch shells so sharp, they cut like knives. To tribes without mesquite trees, he traded mesquite beans, prized as food and medicine. Returning to the coast, he brought animal skins, red ochre for use as face paint, and flint and canes for bows and arrows.

Meanwhile, there was no end to the problems Cabeza de Vaca encountered in what he called "this journeying business," as he roamed alone across Texas and as far north as present-day Oklahoma. He almost starved to death. He almost died of thirst. Lightning nearly hit him. He nearly died of hypothermia. He was in constant danger from predators, both animals and humans.

But somehow, Cabeza de Vaca always endured, and through it all, he kept his sense of himself intact. He had a mission and a dream — not just to reunite with his own people, but to write a report to the king of Spain about the people he met and the places he passed through.

To that end, Cabeza de Vaca memorized every detail he could. No matter how hungry, cold, tired, or endangered he was, he looked around. He watched. He listened. He learned. In so doing, he became the first anthropologist in what is now the American West.

From today's perspective, one of Cabeza de Vaca's most

startling — and poignant — observations was that many tribes in the regions he was passing through led a terribly difficult existence even before Europeans arrived. Some devoted all their energy to gathering food every day of their lives, not even taking time to fabricate such basic essentials as mats. Still, they lived in constant danger of starving. People went three days or more without eating.

Even when they had enough to eat, their diet was badly out of balance. For three months of the year, the Capoques had nothing to eat but oysters. Farther inland, other natives went for several months eating nothing but prickly pear fruits. Because of the great scarcity of food, women in many tribes nursed their children until they were 12 years old to keep them from starving to death or becoming invalids from malnutrition. When they did stop nursing, children had to find enough food for themselves or die.

With too many people and too few resources, tribes in the plains and hills and along the coast warred constantly. As time passed, and Cabeza de Vaca's reputation spread before him, first as a businessman, then as a medicine man, he found that people were so eager to see him, they made peace for his sake. In that way, he became a peacemaker, too. Once again, as he had when he worked as a slave, Cabeza de Vaca was taking on a role the natives usually assigned to women.

Cabeza de Vaca had long been fascinated by women's roles and women's actions. Through all that had happened, he had never forgotten that on the voyage from Spain to the Caribbean, one of the women aboard ship had prophesied that most or all of the explorers with Narváez would meet disaster. If any did survive, she said, astonishing things would happen to them. Now, years later, as he wandered among the Indians, he found himself particularly intrigued by women's roles and their tribulations.

Among the Mariames and Yquaces peoples, he observed, women were forbidden to marry men of their own tribe. But this custom had developed in better times, before food shortages and chronic wars. Now fathers worried that if their daughters married men from other tribes, as they must, their daughters' children would go to war against their mother's own tribe.

The solution: Immediately after birth, infant girls were thrown to the dogs. The starving animals devoured them.

Cabeza de Vaca begged them to stop the practice. He urged parents to allow girls to marry within their own tribe. But he was told, "It is a disgusting thing to marry relatives. It is far better to kill our daughters than to have to give them to either relatives or enemies."

To offset the resulting gender imbalance, men bought wives from other tribes: A wife cost a bow and two arrows, or, lacking that, a man could buy her for a 35-square-foot piece of netting.

These purchased wives were virtual slaves. They had to haul all the wood and water needed for their households. Before dawn, they got up and heated the ovens; at first light, they were out digging roots to bake. Every two or three days, they would take down their mat houses and haul them on their backs as the whole village moved on in search of food.

Even among tribes with more humane customs and beliefs, women worked incessantly. In some cultures, their duties lightened only when they menstruated. Because it was considered unsafe to eat food touched by a menstruating woman, during that time women gathered food only for themselves.

Some cultures celebrated ritual three-day fasts during which people drank tea constantly, from morning to night, about five gallons a day apiece. When someone shouted, "Who wants a drink?" every woman within hearing distance had to freeze in place, even if she had a heavy burden on her back. The natives believed any movement she made would cause the tea to poison its drinkers.

As Cabeza de Vaca fought hunger, assassins, sickness, and the elements, and struggled to keep his head clear enough to observe and remember cultural and geographic details, he returned each year to the island to beg Lope de Oviedo to leave.

In November 1532, Oviedo finally agreed. Taking along some people from Oviedo's adopted tribe, the two men left the island and crossed four rivers along the coast. That alone proved enormously difficult, because Oviedo could not swim.

As the two Spaniards moved in what they hoped was the general direction of Spanish settlements, they reached a bay that was more than two miles across and very deep. The Indian men from Oviedo's island stayed behind, but the two Spanish travelers and some Indian women forded the bay in the shallows. When the Indians they encountered on the far side learned where they were going, they said that farther on there was nothing to eat. The people were so poor, they had no animal skins to cover them, and they were dying from the cold.

But their hosts had good news of sorts, too. Only a few days away lived people like Cabeza de Vaca and Oviedo. Years earlier, many of the shipwrecked survivors had died of hunger and cold, the Indians said. They themselves and members of neighboring tribes had murdered most of the rest. Now only three survived.

"How are they doing?" Cabeza de Vaca asked.

Not well, was the answer. They were slaves; the boys and men they lived among amused themselves by kicking, hitting, and battering them.

To show Cabeza de Vaca and Oviedo what they meant, the Indians slapped them, hit them, and threw dirt clods at them. They held arrows to the travelers' hearts and said, "Maybe we should kill you the way we killed your friends."

When the Indians had finished, Oviedo said, "I want to go back to my island."

This time Cabeza de Vaca could not convince him to change his mind. The women from Oviedo's adopted tribe set out to rejoin their husbands, and Oviedo went with them. The last that Cabeza de Vaca saw of his friend, he and the Indian women were wading along the shoreline of the bay, in the direction of home.

At that moment, Oviedo earned a place in history as the

first known European to choose to settle permanently in what is now the American West.

Because of Oviedo, Cabeza de Vaca had stayed on in Texas far longer than he needed to. Now he headed off to find the other survivors.

The first, Alonso del Castillo Maldonado, was a native of Salamanca and the son of a physician. The second, Andrés Dorantes, had survived the shipwreck with his brother, but the people who lived along the bay had murdered his brother "for sport."

The third, named simply Estevánico, was not a Spaniard at all, but what Cabeza de Vaca called "an Arabian Black." A native of Azemmour in north Africa, Estevánico had traveled to the New World as a slave. According to the thinking of the day, in spite of their changed circumstances, Estevánico still belonged to Dorantes.

Dorantes was ready to flee, if they could, but like Oviedo before them, Castillo and Estevánico didn't want to leave.

Presumably, Cabeza de Vaca could have returned to his solitary wandering as a merchant, while he waited for his companions. But he may have been too lonely; he allowed himself to be enslaved again, this time by the same family that owned Dorantes.

Finally, in September 1534, the four men escaped. It was now that Cabeza de Vaca developed his role of medicine man and healer. With time, his three companions became healers, too. Perhaps medical knowledge Castillo absorbed as a child from his father helped the men. Again and again, the patients the four treated pronounced themselves cured.

As the naked men walked inland across the continent, they drew huge crowds. Cabeza de Vaca, who otherwise seldom bragged, said later of his medical work, "I was the boldest and most venturous in trying to cure anything." Sometimes he used a popular native technique of cutting the skin above the pain, sucking the wound, and cauterizing it. When forced to, he even performed surgery. One time he cut open a man's chest with a flint knife, removed an enormous arrowhead that was lodged sideways above the heart, then stitched the wound shut. The patient recovered quickly, and the natives celebrated "with their customary dances and festivals."

Twice a year, the four naked travelers shed their skins like snakes. By this time they had adapted so well to hunger that even when food was more plentiful, they ate only once a day, in the evening. Their favorite food, a full day's ration, was a single handful of deer tallow. Apart from the sores that covered them, they remained astonishingly healthy.

It is said that in their final 240 days of actual travel, the four companions walked more than 2,400 miles. By the time they encountered Spanish soldiers, in March 1536, they had left what is now the American Southwest and reached Sinaloa, Mexico, near the Pacific Ocean. At first, the 600 Indians who accompanied them refused to believe that their four wild-looking but wise companions could possibly be Spaniards like the soldiers. The pilgrims healed the sick, while the Spaniards killed the healthy. The pilgrims traveled barefoot and naked; the Spaniards traveled clothed, armed, and mounted on horses. The pilgrims gave away all they had; the Spaniards robbed everyone they met. Even Cabeza de Vaca couldn't believe the difference. One of the first things he did, upon reuniting with his countrymen, was to protect the Indians who traveled with him from being seized and sold to Spanish settlers as slaves.

By now Cabeza de Vaca was about 46. His years in the wilderness must have aged him externally, but his lust for adventure remained intact. He returned to his compatriots feeling vital, invigorated, and ready for action.

Although Cabeza de Vaca left New Spain (Mexico) soon afterward, he continued to lead an adventure-filled life. He fled French pirates. He walked barefoot through the jungles of South America. When he insisted on fair treatment for natives there, his enemies returned him in chains to Spain. After years of fighting to reclaim his honor, he died a hero in his late 60s.

But his most enduring achievement was to write his

long-dreamed-of report to the king. First published in 1542, *Adventures in the Unknown Interior of America* has been a classic ever since, and it remains in print today. Part true-life adventure story, part non-fiction novel, it is above all an anthropology report, a collection of observances about the cultures and lifeways of the people he encountered.

Despite his careful attention to detail, Cabeza de Vaca left scholars a conundrum. In eight years of wandering in the wilderness, he visited dozens of tribes and walked at least 5,000 miles. Who were these people, and what was his route as he traveled back to New Spain?

We know he started in Texas. Moreover, Coronado's men later met Indians on the Great Plains, probably in Oklahoma or the Texas Panhandle, who said that Cabeza de Vaca and his companions had passed their way. And in 1582, Antonio de Espejo met Indians in northern Chihuahua, Mexico, who said that the four men had traveled through the area. So they could have crossed the eastern part of New Mexico before cutting south, but they almost certainly didn't reach present-day Arizona. However, scholars have proposed dozens of possible routes.

What matters most is not Cabeza de Vaca's route, but his tribulations and his courage. His adventures in the West have never been surpassed. He saw what no European before him had seen. He did what no European before him had done. Almost everywhere he went, he and his companions were the first non-Indians the natives had seen. He was the first in a long line of anthropologists to study native cultures of the West and to report on native women's roles. He learned six native languages and adapted so thoroughly to the native lifestyle that when he finally returned to the world of clothing and beds, he found it painful to wear clothes and could sleep only on the bare floor.

Above all, Cabeza de Vaca was the first to give the West its archetypal hero: the enterprising adventurer, down on his luck, who survives every misfortune and disaster that nature, fate, and other humans bombard him with.

During his travels, he came to cherish and respect native peoples as few after him did. Following his return, he taught love, kindness, and accommodation toward the people who already populated the Americas. Yet his report and his travels turned Spanish attention to the north, to what is now the American West, resulting in great hardships and upheavals for the natives.

In that respect, Cabeza de Vaca became not just the West's first triumphant survivor, but also its first tragic hero.

# Francisco Vázquez de Coronado

## Lured by Lies, He Searches for Gold

*People have pictured Coronado
as the archetypal greedy explorer, driven
by lust for gold. But Coronado, who was
barely 30 when he set out, came to see himself
as truth-seeker, myth-smasher, and commander
of the world's largest verification squad.
Like truth-seekers before and after him,
he grew darkly pessimistic.*

W HEN SHIPWRECK SURVIVOR ALVAR NÚÑEZ CABEZA DE Vaca finally reached New Spain (Mexico), he reported that the mountainous areas he passed through gave signs of holding gold, silver, and other metals. That led the viceroy, the King's representative in New Spain, to send Fray Marcos de Niza northward in 1539 into what now is Arizona and New Mexico. The friar reported seeing a vast metropolis larger than Mexico City and hearing stories of "much gold." Rumors mushroomed until it was said that Fray Marcos had found a fabulous land called Cíbola, the Seven Cities of Gold.

At that point it seemed as if the collective will of all New Spain were pushing for another expedition northward. Francisco Vázquez de Coronado, the young son-in-law of one of New Spain's most powerful politicians, was chosen as leader. But even in those days, it cost a lot of money to go exploring, in any fashion short of that followed by Cabeza de Vaca and his friends during their ordeal. At a time when the highest-paid

**EMBARKING ON HIS QUEST FOR GOLD,
CORONADO ALSO FELT OBLIGATED
TO FIND THE TRUTH.**

professionals earned no more than 1,500 ducats annually, the viceroy contributed 60,000 ducats — more than $5 million by today's reckoning — toward outfitting 300 or more European explorers and hundreds of natives. Coronado's wife mortgaged her property. Other wealthy people contributed, too. It was their era's version of venture capitalism.

Within a few months of setting out, Coronado proved that Cíbola was only a collection of adobe villages, home to the Zuni Indians. The Zunis owned garnets and turquoise, but no gold. One of Coronado's soldiers, Pedro de Castañeda, who more than 20 years later wrote the most detailed surviving chronicle of the expedition, called Cíbola "a little, unattractive village, looking as if it had been crumpled all up together." Coronado himself wrote to the viceroy in August 1540, "God knows that I wish I had better news to write to Your Lordship, but I must give you the truth."

Soon afterward, Coronado's explorers settled into a winter camp at Tiguex, along the Río Grande near present-day Albuquerque, New Mexico. There, they heard stories of a fabulously wealthy country or countries called Harale or Quivira, 900 miles to the east or north.

The storyteller was a Plains Indian, a slave of the Pueblo Indians at Pecos, north of the Spaniards' winter camp. The explorers nicknamed him el Turco, the Turk, because they thought he looked Turkish.

According to el Turco, villages in Harale were much larger and houses were much finer than those of the Pueblo Indians. Its rulers ate on plates made of gold. They rang enormous golden bells. They traveled in mammoth, canopy-covered canoes ornamented with gold on rivers that held fish as large as horses. Even ordinary people lived in an elegant, refined manner. Indeed, el Turco assured the Spaniards, Harale ranked as the most marvelous and wealthiest place on the continent.

Coronado didn't believe el Turco, he wrote to the king. But he felt he owed it to His Majesty to investigate the Indian's claims.

As soon as the weather warmed, Coronado led more than 1,500 men, women, and children eastward in search of Harale. El Turco accompanied the expedition, as did another Plains Indian guide named Ysopete. The enormous caravan included African servants and slaves, who brought their sea nets along, in case they reached the sea.

"El Turco is lying," Ysopete warned. Coronado believed Ysopete but had to see for himself. Meanwhile, the other soldiers fawned over el Turco and ignored Ysopete.

For more than a month, the travelers pushed eastward across the plains, averaging about 17 miles a day. To guide the main army across the flatness with no landmarks, an advance guard piled buffalo dung into cairns.

Day after day, the explorers slogged forward, their stomachs churning at the sudden change in diet: They had eaten the last corn; only meat remained. What scant water they found was muddy.

In the Texas Panhandle, or thereabouts, an advance party encountered Indians who said Cabeza de Vaca and his comrades had passed through the area. The Indians told stories about the healing powers of the pilgrims. One Indian woman had a daughter, presumably the offspring of Cabeza de Vaca or one of his companions, with skin "as white as a Castilian lady," but with her chin painted Indian style.

One afternoon, while the explorers rested in a ravine, a thunderstorm pounded the encampment with hailstones the size of bowls. The soldiers tried to ward off the stones with helmets and shields. The Africans threw their sea nets over some horses to protect them. Other horses scrambled right up the side of the ravine, trying to escape the hail.

The frozen balls pounded the crockery so hard that every plate and pot broke. The hail pummeled the gourds — essential for food storage and transport — into uselessness. It shredded tents, wounded horses, and dented helmets and shields.

The tattered explorers moved on, where they found an even deeper ravine, possibly Palo Duro Canyon. A stream ran through it. Along the banks grew mulberries, walnuts, roses, grapes, and wild prunes.

Compared to the monotonous countryside they had been passing through, this spot seemed like paradise.

As Coronado always did, he questioned the Indians he encountered in the canyon. Until now, the responses had been equivocal, perhaps because el Turco got to the informants before Coronado did. But this time, the Indians agreed with Ysopete. There was no city overflowing with silver and gold.

Somewhere to the north lay a place called Quivira, but its houses were made of straw, and its wealth consisted of corn.

Pondering this report, Coronado decided that although he needed to see this elusive kingdom with his own eyes, he didn't need to drag the whole army along. Selecting 30 horsemen and a few foot soldiers, he ordered the rest to return to the Río Grande and wait.

They didn't want to go back. Adventurers to the core, they told him they'd rather continue on, even if that meant dying. When Coronado left, still refusing, they sent messengers after him, begging him to reconsider.

While they waited to hear from Coronado, the persistent would-be explorers ventured from camp to hunt buffalo and often lost their way because the land was so flat. Each night, those who made it back to camp fired off guns to guide those who had failed to return. They blew trumpets. They beat drums and built huge fires. Still, sometimes lost hunters spent two or three days finding their way back.

They lacked compasses, and when they grew disoriented during the day, they had to wait to see where the sun set to regain their sense of direction. They couldn't even follow their own tracks because the grass that covered the prairie sprang back immediately after being stepped on, leaving no trace of their passing. One man never did find his way back. Two horses, saddled and bridled, disappeared, too.

Admiringly, the men watched how the natives kept track of direction. When the sun rose, showing them where east lay, they turned in the direction they wanted to travel and shot an arrow straight ahead as far as it would go. It entered the earth and served as a marker. Before they reached that arrow, they shot another straight beyond it, and so on all day, until they arrived at their destination.

Meanwhile, Coronado sent back messengers restating his original orders: The travelers must return to the Río Grande.

Two decades had passed since Magellan's ships circled the earth, but many people still believed North America was part of

# Francisco Vázquez de Coronado

**CORONADO LED AN EXPEDITION OF SOLDIERS, INDIANS, FAMILIES, SLAVES, AND PRIESTS.**

Asia. As the bulk of Coronado's army rode and walked back toward Tiguex, they wondered if explorer Marco Polo had passed this way on his trip to China. Like him, they had encountered cows with humps and people who used dogs as pack animals.

Following the needle of his compass, Coronado and his companions traveled north for more than 40 days. Ysopete grew happier and happier. He was going home.

By the time the explorers reached Quivira, the soldier whose job it was to measure distances each day reported that they had traveled more than 900 miles, putting them somewhere in present-day Kansas.

People received the long-lost Ysopete and his exotic companions happily, and Coronado immediately got down to the business of fact-checking. For 25 days he and his men traveled from village to village until they knew for certain that Ysopete spoke the truth. The natives possessed neither silver nor gold. They lived in round houses made of straw in small villages — 25 in all. From a European standpoint, the most valuable item any of them possessed was a lone copper plate, which their ruler wore around his neck. Like the Comanches and other Plains Indians, the villagers ate raw meat. Although they planted corn and lived in settled villages, they lacked cotton and made all their clothes from buffalo hides.

One soldier, who perhaps had believed el Turco's tales, wrote that the Quivirans were "without decency whatever in their houses nor in anything." Even Coronado expressed disappointment that they didn't fit his definition of civilized, but he was pleased when their leader gave him the neck plate, which he saved to send to the viceroy.

Mostly, though, the Quivirans puzzled and intrigued Coronado. The women didn't resemble Indian women he had seen elsewhere, he said, but looked more like Moorish women. At 6½ feet tall, the men stood a head and more higher than their Spanish visitors.

By Coronado's calculations, he had reached the 40th parallel and Mexico City lay about 2,500 miles to the south. If he was right, he had arrived at the present-day boundary between Nebraska and Kansas. Some scholars place him even farther north, among the Pawnee in Nebraska.

When Coronado confronted el Turco about his lie, the man claimed that his masters at Pecos Pueblo had put him up to luring the Spaniards onto the plains, where their provisions would give out and they would die. Or, if they somehow managed to return to Pueblo country, they would be so weak that the Pueblo Indians could kill them easily, despite the Spaniards' superior weapons.

His confession made, el Turco urged the Quivirans to attack the Spaniards. When the exasperated soldiers learned about this new betrayal, they looped a rope around his neck and twisted it tighter and tighter until he died.

Before leaving Quivira, Coronado erected a large wooden cross. Into the base he chiseled, "Francisco Vázquez de Coronado, general of the army, arrived here."

Coronado said good-bye to Ysopete, who chose to stay among his people.

Guided by six young men from Quivira, Coronado and his men returned by a much shorter, more direct route to the Río Grande. There, on October 20, 1541, Coronado wrote to the king again. "What I am sure of is that there is not any gold or any other metal in all that country." Not in Quivira. Not along the Río Grande. Not anywhere that his men had explored.

On that point, Coronado was wrong, and Cabeza de Vaca was right. The mountains of the West did indeed abound in gold, silver, copper, and other minerals. Less than 50 miles from Tiguex, within sight of Coronado's route to Pecos Pueblo, lay the gold-rich Ortiz Mountains and what would become the Cerrillos Mining District, source of copper, silver, manganese, malachite, and lead.

But Coronado's biggest error lay in deciding that this remarkable new land was unlivable. The best place he had found in all his travels, he told the king, was the Pueblo Indian country of the Río Grande. Even so, he wrote, "It would not be possible to establish a settlement here." The area was too remote, he explained, and the winters too cold.

His facts all neatly verified to his own satisfaction, Coronado returned home to New Spain the following spring, never dreaming that parts of northern New Mexico, the very area he considered unlivable, might someday become some of the most fashionable addresses in the West. But time has proved the West's first fact-checker more pessimistic than right.

# CHAPTER THREE

# The Forgotten First Colonists

## Splinters from Coronado's Band Hang On

*On the November day in 1532 when
Lope de Oviedo told Alvar Núñez Cabeza
de Vaca good-bye, Oviedo became the
first-known European to settle in what now is
the American West. A decade later, members
of Coronado's expedition stayed behind to face
the unknown with courage, foolhardiness,
and daring. Like Oviedo, who survived a
shipwreck and took up residence on an island,
they have vanished from memory.*

---

SOON AFTER CORONADO'S RETURN FROM QUIVIRA TO TIGUEX on the Río Grande, the explorers took a break to celebrate the feast day of a saint. Coronado and a friend challenged each other to a horse race. Coronado selected a particularly powerful horse, and as the servants saddled it, they decided on impulse to use a new girth to cinch the saddle in place.

The two riders charged forward. Coronado pulled ahead by a horse length or more.

Suddenly, the new girth broke and Coronado crashed to the ground.

His friend was so close behind that he could neither stop his horse nor veer away. One of the hooves slammed into the general's head, almost killing him.

The wound took months to heal. One day, while Coronado lay in bed in a gloomy mood, he recalled a forgotten incident when a friend in Spain had predicted that Coronado would become a powerful lord in distant lands but would have a fall from which he would not recover.

Holding his bandaged head, the injured leader longed to see his wife and children. He decided it was time to take the explorers home.

Some officers tried to change Coronado's mind, but he refused to listen. He preferred to face angry investors, who had gambled their money on riches he couldn't find, than to stay where he was and die or to continue searching for wealth he was convinced didn't exist.

In the two years since leaving their homes in New Spain (Mexico), many people had grown to love this strange and remarkable land. They came to the general's bedside to ask permission to stay.

One of the first was a lay Franciscan friar named Luís de Escalona.

"I am an old man," he said, "and I will probably die soon anyway." He wanted to spend whatever time remained to him bringing Christianity to the Indians of Pecos Pueblo.

Neither the subsequent written record nor the oral history of the Indians suggests that they had the slightest desire to be converted, but Escalona believed they did. He asked Coronado only that a young boy named Christopher, a slave belonging to Capt. Juan de Jaramillo, be allowed to accompany him, "to be his consolation" and to learn the language of Pecos Pueblo and interpret for the friar.

Coronado granted Fray Luís's request and ordered soldiers to accompany the old man and the young slave boy to Pecos. The friar took along a chisel and adze so that he could erect crosses at Pecos and other pueblos.

When they heard that Fray Luís would remain behind, a black man and his wife and children — slaves belonging to Melchior Pérez — asked for and received permission to stay, too. So did some Mexican Indians and another of Jaramillo's African slaves, one named Sebastián.

An additional 60 explorers announced to the ill leader that they did not want to go back. Among them was a Spanish woman, Francisca de Hozes.

When Coronado heard the dissenters' demands, he put them in shackles and threatened to hang them. At least, that's what Señora de Hozes told authorities later.

Scholars doubt the señora's account, if only because the expedition didn't carry that many shackles. But it is clear that doña Francisca fumed when she and her husband and friends couldn't stay with Fray Luís.

She was luckier than she realized. Shortly before Coronado headed back to New Spain, he sent messengers to take a small flock of sheep to Fray Luís. The men encountered the lay pastor traveling with some Indians from Pecos. He was on his way to preach to people in another village about 50 miles away, he said. He also told the messengers that the old men of Pecos — the spiritual leaders — were already deserting him. He believed they would kill him soon. Surely they would have responded similarly to a high-spirited, independent-minded Spanish woman bent on doing as she pleased.

Meanwhile, another friar, Juan de Padilla, petitioned Coronado for permission to stay. Nicknamed "The Fighting Friar," Fray Juan had been a frontiersman and soldier before he joined the Coronado expedition. Since then, he had taken one side trip to Hopi country and another to Taos Pueblo. He had been one of the first to meet el Turco and to hear his story of a fabulous land of great wealth, off to the north or east. He had also been one of Coronado's close advisors. Most important, he had already walked all the way to Kansas and back with Coronado. The friar in Padilla wanted nothing more than to return to Quivira and bring the gospel to the natives, but it appears that the adventurer in him also longed to continue searching for mythical cities, and gold.

When Coronado told Fray Juan he could stay, the priest packed his candles and other religious supplies. Andrés do Campo, a Portuguese gardener turned soldier, offered to escort Fray Juan. Two lay brothers, who were Mexican Indians, wanted to go, too. A free African man, unnamed in the record, offered to act as an interpreter, and various servants also stayed. Coronado provided pack mules, a flock of sheep, gifts for the Indians, and the six guides from Quivira who had accompanied Coronado's expedition back to the Rio Grande.

Rather than wandering across the plains, as they had under el Turco's direction the previous year, Fray Juan and his companions followed the short, direct route. The sheep slowed them down, so that they probably traveled only about 15 miles a day. Even so, the travelers reached Quivira about May of 1542, not long after Coronado and the other explorers started homeward from Tiguex.

Near the site where Coronado had erected his farewell cross, probably somewhere in central Kansas, Fray Juan set up a mission station. To the Quivirans he was an old acquaintance, if not an old friend. They accepted him and the others and allowed him to preach the gospel and teach their children.

Probably, Fray Juan could have stayed in Quivira and lived to an ancient age, and we would never have known what became of him. But once he grew used to Quivira, he longed to set out again and explore. The Quivirans begged him not to venture eastward, where their enemies lived. Such a journey would not be safe even for them, they said, much less for a stranger like him.

Fray Juan ignored them. Taking do Campo and the two Mexican lay brothers and some servants, he started walking eastward. Do Campo brought the only horse.

News of their approach reached the Quivirans' enemies, and a party of warriors headed west to intercept them.

When Fray Juan saw the warriors, he ordered do Campo to take the two Mexican Indians and flee.

**THE EXPEDITION'S INVESTORS FUMED WHEN
CORONADO RETURNED EARLY — AND WITHOUT GOLD.**

At first they wouldn't leave, but he insisted.

Then Fray Juan, the Fighting Friar, fell on his knees and prayed, offering his soul to God.

The Indians shot so many arrows, that when his fleeing companions looked back, feathered shafts appeared to fill his entire body.

Surviving accounts contradict each other, but it appears that the attackers let the two Mexican Indians escape and captured do Campo and his horse. In a rerun of Cabeza de Vaca's story, the Quivirans' enemies forced the former Portuguese gardener to work as a slave.

It isn't known what happened to the free African and the servants who accompanied Fray Juan to Quivira. Later travelers found no trace of them, their descendants, or Fray Juan's sheep and mules.

Do Campo survived. Ten months after Fray Juan's death, he escaped and began the long walk back to New Spain in the company of two dogs. The two lay brothers also walked to New Spain, but it isn't known whether the three traveled separately or together. Either way, do Campo carried a cross as he wandered. So did the others. The Indians that do Campo met in Oklahoma and Texas — people who had known or heard of Alvar Núñez Cabeza de Vaca — welcomed do Campo, accepted his blessings, and gave him food.

Traveling almost due south, do Campo arrived at Pánuco, near present-day Tampico, Mexico, several years later. His hair and beard had grown so long, they hung in matted braids. By March of 1547, the former captive reached Mexico City, where his adventures became the biggest news of the day.

Politicos and investors still hadn't forgiven Coronado for returning home so soon and so empty-handed. There is no evidence that do Campo claimed to have found or seen gold, but his return started people in New Spain dreaming again. They would send another exploring party north, they decided, this time directly to Quivira, along do Campo's escape route.

Meanwhile, the two lay brothers reached their home monastery, in western Mexico. One died soon afterwards, but the other lived many years, presumably telling tales of his wanderings and the people he encountered in the far north.

The years passed, and no news reached New Spain from Fray Luís de Escalona, back at Pecos Pueblo. As those who had left him behind in the north grew old, they sat in their homes in Mexico and wondered and worried about him.

One of Coronado's former comrades, Pedro de Castañeda, was still thinking of Fray Luís in the 1560s and trying to guess his fate. Castañeda preferred not to believe the friar's prediction that he would be murdered. The friar had been "a man of good and saintly life," Castañeda wrote in his belated report of Coronado's journey. Moreover, the Pueblo Indians were merciful, opposed to cruelty, and loyal to their friends. Surely, he reasoned, God must have allowed Fray Luís to live long enough to convert some Indians and train a successor to take over after his death.

As the decades passed, and the people who had known Fray Luís died, the tradition grew that the old friar had lived in a cave or a hut. It was said that the Indians kept him alive by bringing him beans, tortillas, and a native drink called *atole*, made from ground corn.

That's probably wishful thinking. Given the friar's premonition before Coronado left, and the fact that other friars who stayed alone among the Pueblos in the early 1580s were quickly murdered, it is likely that Fray Luís died a martyr at the hands of exasperated Indians who grew tired of his demands that they accept Christianity.

The Mexican Indians whom Coronado left behind fared better. They settled among the Pueblo Indians, intermarried, and assimilated. Some moved to Zuni. Three were still living when Antonio de Espejo visited Zuni in 1583: Gaspar from Mexico City, Andrés from Cuyuacán, and Antón from Guadalajara. When don Juan de Oñate visited Zuni in 1598, he met Gaspar's son Alonso. The man spoke no Spanish and remembered only a few words of his father's native Nahuatl.

As in the case of Lope de Oviedo, the Spanish castaway who settled off the Texas coast, nothing further is known of what happened to the former slave named Sebastián or to the little slave boy Christopher who stayed with Fray Luís.

The anonymous black man who stayed behind in New Mexico with his wife and children disappeared from the record the day Coronado headed south. Whoever they were, whatever their names, this family of former slaves — a man, his wife, two children or more — were the first non-Indian family to settle in what now is the American West.

# The Pirate Francis Drake

## Bold Englishman Steals California

*In the days when Europeans considered the Pacific Ocean a vast Spanish lake, the young Francis Drake made fame and fortune by becoming the first English pirate to reach the Pacific. Known to his victims as Francisco Draque, he plundered, kidnapped, and robbed until his ship grew so heavy, he couldn't carry another vara of silk. Then he performed one final act of piracy: stealing California.*

---

IN 1527, SPANISH SHIPS BEGAN TRAVELING BACK AND FORTH between Acapulco, Mexico, and the Philippines. To the Philippines they carried weapons, tools, ammunition, and other items in a four-month voyage. The ships, called *naos de China*, or Manila galleons, brought porcelain, fine china, silks, cinnamon, other spices, gold, and much more back to New Spain (Mexico).

The fastest return route lay in an arching path that took advantage of trade winds and currents and carried ships far to the north, to the coast off present-day Monterey, California. Even so, the heavy cargoes slowed the ships, and the return voyage took six months.

Conditions aboard ship were nightmarish. Sailors grew hungry, sick, thirsty, cold. All sorts of vermin, from roaches to rats, overran the men's beds, their food, and even their bodies.

**DRAKE'S VOYAGE MADE HIM AND HIS CREW
THE FIRST ENGLISHMEN TO
CIRCUMNAVIGATE THE GLOBE.**

Still, a single ship could carry a lifetime fortune — as much as $32 million in today's money.

As news of this wealth reached Europe, political leaders and their sometime allies — pirates — coveted galleons' cargoes. But maps were state secrets, and whole oceans were off limits to ships flying the wrong flag. The Portuguese controlled the Indian Ocean, preventing other nations' ships from entering — or leaving — the Pacific from the west. Spanish ships patrolled approaches to the Strait of Magellan, at the tip of South America, allowing no one into the Pacific from the east. From a European standpoint, such controls turned the Pacific into an enormous Spanish lake.

In that century of one astonishing discovery after another, it still was believed universally that an undiscovered third route to the Pacific existed. The Spanish called it the Strait of Anián. Somewhere north of explored territory, the undiscovered strait was said to link the Pacific directly with the north Atlantic. The navigator who found it would win great honor — and a great fortune — by claiming it for his country.

In his youth, the notorious English pirate Francis Drake longed to be that man. By 1571, he had been sailing for nearly 20 years but was only about 30 years old. Twice already, he had reached the West Indies, and both times the proud Protestant came away feeling humiliated by Catholic Spanish authorities who matter-of-factly required the hot-headed youth to obey Spanish law. Reflecting his era's racist, Anglo-centric thinking, known as *la leyenda negra*, or the Black Legend, Drake considered Spaniards by their very nature to be evil and cruel.

In 1572, the red-haired pirate, whom the Spanish called Francisco Draque, retaliated by plundering Nombre de Dios in Panama. From there, Draque reportedly traveled overland until he could view the Pacific. Staring at the forbidden waters, he vowed to enter them and continue seeking revenge: for himself, for God, for the queen.

However, England's Queen Elizabeth and Spain's King Felipe II declared a truce, and Drake had to wait. But after the truce dissolved, Drake set out in December 1577 on the most adventurous and daring voyage of his career.

From the moment he left English waters, Drake plundered: three caravels here, a ship there, crops and supplies. He even kidnapped a Portuguese pilot to guide him through the Strait of Magellan. In August 1578, in the middle of fierce winter storms, Drake slipped undetected through the strait into the Pacific Ocean and headed north along the South American coast.

No pirate before him had ever reached the Pacific, and the colonists lived unprotected and unprepared. To Drake's advantage, news traveled more slowly than ships. Again and again, he simply showed up and stole. At one port, he found a Spaniard sleeping by the sea with 23 bars of silver, worth about 6,000 silver pesos, lying unguarded beside him. "We tooke the silver, and left the man," notes an anonymous report of the voyage published in England in 1600.

Exuberantly, the pirate looted his way northward, plundering coastal towns, ships, people, churches. His booty ranged from two llamas, loaded with silver, to an entire ship heavy with jewels, precious stones, gold, Chinese silks, and 26 tons of silver.

In Valparaiso, Chile, the pirates kidnapped Juan Griego, "Juan the Greek," the pilot of a Spanish ship. Off Costa Rica, they captured two pilots who knew the Spanish galleons' routes. But by now Drake's ship, the *Pelican*, had grown too heavy with booty to carry another yard of Chinese silk, and the pirate decided he had avenged himself enough. Besides, the men had been gone for over a year and longed to return home.

Drake knew he couldn't retrace his route. Every Spanish ship along the South American coast would be looking for him. He considered heading out across the Pacific. But off the coast of southern Mexico, near present-day Acapulco, he found his ship becalmed. The situation seemed perfect for Drake to search for the Strait of Anián.

Making occasional stops, the pirates-turned-explorers headed toward the "pole Arctike."

In a vague way, these waters were already known. Bartolomé Ferrer had sailed at least as far north as the 42nd parallel — today's Oregon-California border — in 1543. But eventually Drake's ship reached waters that in the past probably had seen only Indian canoes and an occasional off-course Manila galleon. Drake and his men estimated later that they traveled between 2,000 and 4,800 miles northward from New Spain along the coast.

Wherever they were, by June 1579, the air had grown unendurably cold, even for Englishmen.

"The raine which fell, was an unnatural congealed and frozen substance," wrote Francis Fletcher, a minister who accompanied the expedition. When they removed meat from the fire, it froze. The ropes stiffened, and six men could barely do what three had done easily before. Even sailors who had explored above the Arctic Circle in Europe said they had never felt such cold in summer.

"A sudden and great discouragement seized upon the mindes of our men," Fletcher wrote.

The pirates wanted to turn back, but Drake wasn't ready. The *Pelican* continued northward.

Later, Fletcher claimed that the ship reached 48 degrees north — off the present-day coast of Washington, just south of the Strait of Juan de Fuca. Another account put the *Pelican* farther south, at roughly the site of present-day Coos Bay, Oregon. Whatever point the *Pelican* reached, the winds changed and pushed it southward.

Staying close to the coast, Drake's sailors saw snow-covered hills and mountains. Twelve days later, on June 17, they found what Fletcher called "a convenient and fit harbor." Another chronicler called it "a faire and good Bay."

Their instruments told them they were just north of 38 degrees, a little north of present-day San Francisco.

By now, worms were eating the ship's planks, and the ship was leaking. The sailors went ashore and, with the help of their black slaves, piled stones into walls to make a sturdy, fort-like enclosure at the base of a hill. Inside, they pitched their tents. Laboriously, they unloaded all the silks, porcelains, spices, silver, gold, jewels, and other plunder and stored them in the enclosure. Then they set to replacing the ship's damaged planks.

It was still so cold, damp, and cloudy that only this strenuous physical labor kept them warm. According to Fletcher, the men congratulated themselves for being so "strong and hardned " and they spoke disparagingly of "chamber champions" — their era's couch potatoes — people "who lye on their feather-beds till they go to sea, or rather whose teeth in a temperate aire do beate in their heads."

The fort lay less than a mile from a native village, where Indians lived in warm, round dugout houses covered with wooden roofs. The natives clustered around these pale, energetic newcomers.

Native men wore fur cloaks, but little else. The women wore buckskin clothes, reed skirts, or nothing at all. They performed a strange, self-mutilating ritual for the strangers. They clawed the skin off their cheeks until the blood ran down their chests. All of them, even those heavily pregnant, threw themselves on the ground again and again, until they grew exhausted. The unnerved pirates countered by praying, singing psalms, and reading the Bible aloud.

A man whom the English took to be the Indians' king removed his own "crown" — made of feathers of many colors — and set it on Drake's head. He took off his own necklaces, made of bone or ivory, and placed them around the pirate's neck. The English concluded that the natives were pledging allegiance to Queen Elizabeth and that they considered the English to be gods.

During the five weeks the pirates stayed among them, the Indians came almost daily to watch them work and listen to them sing. The English fed them and gave them pieces of Chinese damask and other gifts from their bounteous cargo.

By the end of July, the Englishmen had finished their repairs and reloaded their cargo onto the *Pelican*, which Drake at some point rechristened the *Golden Hind*.

On a brass plate the pirates engraved the date of their arrival, the names of Drake and Queen Elizabeth, and a flowery inscription that claimed the region for the queen. Fletcher wrote that they drove "a great and firme post" into the ground and nailed the plate to it, along with a picture of the queen. They also fastened "a peece of six pence of current English money" to the post.

Wistfully, the fair-haired pirates named the entire region New Albion or New England.

In a sense, this was a final, double act of piracy. By today's standards, it seems absurd and a little frightening that they would assume they had the right to take possession of land that already belonged to the Indians. By the standards of their own day, it was just as absurd and frightening, but for a different reason. Following the accepted practices of that era's version of international law, Spanish explorers had already claimed the land in the name of the king of Spain.

The Indians begged them not to leave. But late in July 1579, the *Golden Hind* sailed out of "the faire and good Bay." The Indians watched mournfully from the hilltops and lit signal fires.

By now, Drake doubted that the Strait of Anián existed. If it did, it surely lay too far northward to be navigable. He headed across the Pacific.

Many months and adventures later, most of his loot intact, Drake arrived back in England and quickly became famous. But the queen sealed all his reports and decreed the death penalty to any crew member who revealed Drake's route.

Scholars have been arguing about the details of Drake's plundering voyage ever since. As the historian Harry Kelsey wrote in 1990, "After four centuries of research, nearly every important aspect of the voyage is a matter of uncertainty, contradiction, and dispute."

Some scholars assume that the entire northern part of Drake's voyage is a fabrication. But some accounts suggest it could be true.

In one account, a wild-looking white man, a foreigner identified in the record only as Señor de Morera, arrived in 1583 at the Mexican mining communities of Nueva Vizcaya

— present-day Durango and Chihuahua — with a remarkable tale:

Morera had worked as a pilot for Francisco Draque and traveled far, far to the north with him. Before turning southward, Draque had discovered what appeared to be the Strait of Anián. But at the moment of discovery, Morera fell so ill that the pirates expected him to die. They put him ashore, gambling that the climate on land would be more conducive to survival than conditions aboard ship. Within a few days, Morera did recover. For four years he walked, first heading southward to the Gulf of California, then cutting inland. He estimated that by the time he reached the Gulf of California, he had already walked 1,500 miles.

Unfortunately, Señor de Morera lacked Cabeza de Vaca's zeal to record his adventures, and little more is known of him or his journey.

In 1584, Spaniards captured Juan Draque — John Drake, a young relative of Francis Drake and one of those who had sailed with him. Juan Draque also said the pirates had traveled far to the north, all the way to the 48th parallel.

Finally, comes an account of an expedition in 1602-1603 by Sebastián Vizcaino, who explored and mapped the California coast. At Santa Catalina Island, Indians told Vizcaino's sailors stories of a visit some years earlier by other white men who had black slaves. As proof of the story, an Indian woman showed Vizcaino two pieces of Chinese damask.

The slaves and silk could have come from any Manila galleon. But another piece of evidence pointed to Francisco Draque and his crew or to later pirates. A generation after the pale, fair-haired pirates' departure, there were "white and blond, and very happy" children on the island.

# CHAPTER FIVE

# Antonio de Espejo
## His Quest for Gold and Silver Wanes

*Antonio de Espejo was just the sort of man who
has always arrived in frontier towns. Impulsive
and hot-headed, he wanted to make a new life
for himself without giving up his penchant for
doing things his own way. But isn't that
the frontier's greatest impossible dream?*

W HEN ESPEJO SHOWED UP IN THE ROUGH-AND-TROUBLE
mining communities of Nueva Vizcaya (Mexico's present-day Durango and Chihuahua) in 1582, the
biggest news of the day was the recent return of an expedition from Nuevo México — or San Felipe de Nuevo México, or
Nueva Andalucía, as it was being called.

The first legal expedition into the north since Coronado's
day, its official purpose had been to convert the Pueblo Indians
to Christianity. Two friars had stayed behind, and now their
fellow friars in Nueva Vizcaya worried about the pair's safety.
Dangers lurked in the north; another friar had been murdered
trying to return home on his own. The Nueva Vizcaya friars
wanted someone to go north, find their missing comrades, and
bring them home.

If Espejo had come to the frontier looking for excitement,
he had found it. A middle-aged man of medium height who let
his considerable wealth show, he talked to the local authorities,
and with the friars' help, secured permission, of sorts, to lead
a rescue operation. At his own expense, he recruited and out-
fitted 14 soldiers.

Chances are, Espejo had not told the friars much more

about himself than that he had been born in Córdoba, Spain, and had been working as a cattle trader in the Mexico City area for some time. He might have mentioned that he had formerly worked as a policeman (a "familiar") for the Inquisition and that the part of the work he enjoyed most was talking to the accused heretics he arrested and transported to prison.

Espejo probably didn't tell the friars that he himself had been arrested twice, by civil authorities, once for murder, once as an accomplice to murder. And he surely didn't talk about the time when authorities confiscated some his cattle, and he rushed into the municipal slaughterhouse in Mexico City, with sword in hand, and shouted, "I will kill anyone — or the whole populace of the city for that matter — who may attempt to rob me of my property!"

On November 10, 1582, Espejo and the soldiers headed north, accompanied by at least one friar, some servants, and 115 horses and mules. One soldier, Miguel Sánchez Valenciano, brought his wife, Casilda de Amaya, and two sons, ages one and three. Possibly, families accompanied other soldiers as well.

Preparing for trouble, Espejo brought "quantities" of arms and munitions, along with food and other supplies. He also carried some mineral samples to show the Indians, in hopes of finding mineral wealth.

When the explorers reached the Río Grande Pueblos, they learned that the Indians whom the friars had planned to convert had killed them.

Espejo's job was done. It was time to go home. But like many before and after him, Espejo found himself fascinated by this strange new land he had entered and by the people who inhabited it. Besides, all along the route, he had been showing the mineral samples to Indians. The natives gave vague, but promising responses. Somewhere out there, Espejo was convinced, he could find silver. Maybe even gold.

He persuaded his companions to stay and explore. This was not, strictly speaking, legal. But they were a long way from anyone who would try to enforce the law or would even

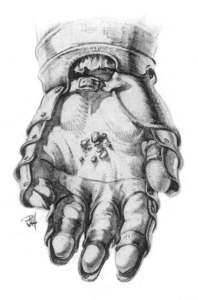

**ESPEJO CARRIED MINERAL SAMPLES
THAT HE HOPED THE INDIANS WOULD RECOGNIZE.**

know that they were violating it. As Espejo rationalized later, "I thought this was a good opportunity for me to serve his Majesty by visiting and exploring the lands so new and so remote, with a view to informing His Majesty about them while incurring no expense to him for their exploration."

For weeks, the Spaniards traveled from one Pueblo Indian village to the next, clearly enchanted by the people and their customs. Espejo marveled at the magpies kept in cages, like birds in Spain, and at the umbrellas, "like Chinese parasols, painted with the sun, the moon, and the stars." He also admired the women, who wore their skirts "like slips, next to the skin, the lower portion loose and swishing."

In March 1583, at Zuni Pueblo, in what now is northwestern New Mexico, the little party found a book and a small trunk left behind by Coronado 40 years earlier. They also met several Mexican Indians who had stayed in New Mexico when Coronado went home. From them Espejo learned what he may not already have known: that Coronado had found neither silver nor gold.

However, the Indians said that much farther on, near the shores of a great lake, gold was abundant. When Coronado's men tried to reach the lake, they ran out of water on the 12th day and could find no more, so they turned back. The lake lay another 48 days' journey — perhaps as much as 1,000 miles — beyond that.

At this point, Espejo's little party of explorers began to argue about what to do next. Casilda de Amaya, who was pregnant again, wanted to go back. So did the friar and five soldiers — four of them relatives of Amaya. Espejo tried to persuade them to stay with him, but as Diego Pérez de Luxán, the expedition's official chronicler, wrote in his journal, "there was much controversy." Finally, Espejo decided to let them leave if they wished.

Nine soldiers, including Pérez de Luxán, remained loyal to him. That was enough, Espejo told himself, as he looked westward, dreaming of that vast lake and its gold.

Accompanied by some Indians from Zuni, the Espejo loyalists started on the well-worn path that led to Hopi country, four days' journey away. But long before they arrived, the Hopis sent a messenger warning them to turn back or be killed.

The Spanish soldiers cut up bright red felt and attached pieces to the heads of the Indians from Zuni, so they could distinguish friends from enemies during battle. Then they continued traveling toward Hopi land in what now is northern Arizona.

When the party reached the Hopi villages, the Indians greeted them peacefully and said they had never wanted to fight. To show their good intentions, they fed the soldiers tortillas, tamales, roasted corn on the cob, and other delicacies. They built a corral to hold the explorers' horses — the first corral in the West. They showered the men with presents: 4,000 cotton blankets, tasseled towels, and more. They sprinkled the explorers and their horses and servants with sacred corn meal — so much that Pérez de Luxán wrote, "We looked like clowns in carnival time."

The Hopi confirmed what people at Zuni had said: Far away lay a great lake near which could be found much gold. However, there were other mines, too, much closer, which the Hopis would be happy to show them.

Espejo left five men behind to transport the gifts back to Zuni. Then, on April 30, he and the remaining four soldiers pushed on.

With Hopis guiding them, the five Spaniards headed directly west for 45 leagues through a mountainous region. Then, incredibly, Espejo found the mines. At least, that was the account he gave when he returned to New Spain.

"I found the mines," he wrote, "and took from them with my own hands ores which, according to experts on the matter, are very rich and contain a great deal of silver."

Never mind that the mines contained silver rather than gold. The find climaxed a dramatic trip.

From the mines, the men returned to Zuni, 70 leagues away, on a more level route than before. To their surprise, Casilda de Amaya and the other dissenters had not left for Nueva Vizcaya. Hoping to convince them to stay, Espejo showed them ores he had taken from the mines. But the dissidents left and even persuaded another soldier to join them.

Having made a major silver strike, Espejo himself could have hurried back to Nueva Vizcaya with the news. Instead, with his dwindling band of loyal followers, he dawdled in the north. He rode out to the buffalo plains and followed the Pecos River south. It was September 20, 1583, before he returned to his starting place in Nueva Vizcaya. Soon afterward, he wrote his report.

Meanwhile, Pérez de Luxán had kept a careful journal, and he submitted it to the authorities in Nueva Vizcaya.

Years later, in 1602, when the viceroy was searching for more information about the wild north, one of his notaries found Pérez de Luxán's chronicle among some old papers.

Pérez de Luxán's report differs significantly from Espejo's regarding the Arizona part of the journey. To begin with, the soldier's journal is much longer and more vivid. He tells of camping the first night out from Hopi, a mere five leagues away, at a dried-up water hole.

"We named this place El Ojo Triste" — Sad Water Hole — he wrote. The next morning, two hours before dawn, they hurried on. By May 5, 1583, on the sixth day of travel, they had reached "a warm land in which there are parrots."

On May 7, they came to an abandoned pueblo, by a marsh. Nearby some natives built a hut of branches for the Spaniards and planted a large painted cross and four small ones outside. Clearly, they had encountered other Spaniards before. Pérez de Luxán wrote, "All the men, women, and children were seated in a row, with their heads low, singing of the peace they wished with us."

To further prove that they wanted peace, these people gave the Spaniards some ores — and offered to take them to the mines. For another four leagues the group traveled. They crossed a large river and climbed into "a very rough sierra." It was May 9, the 10th day since leaving Hopi, when, just as Espejo reported, they found the mines.

But in Pérez de Luxán's telling, the mines were "so worthless that we did not find in any of them a trace of silver, as they were copper mines, and poor."

One man, probably Espejo, was lying — surely not prompted by malice, perhaps not even greed, but by the common human need to put the best light possible on what he had seen and done.

Modern scholars quibble about the details of Espejo's expedition — which route the men took and where the mines lay — but for the non-scholar, the significance of Espejo's ventures lies elsewhere.

Change had taken place in the impetuous former policeman while he traveled around the north. He had fallen in love, not with real or imaginary mines, but with a place, that great, wild, and glorious expanse of land that we know today as the American West.

Espejo returned to Nueva Vizcaya with a dream: to go back, this time to stay. On April 23, 1584, he wrote a letter directly to King Felipe II, asking for permission to return and establish a colony.

"I beg . . . that it may be your pleasure for me to spend the rest of my life in the continuation of these discoveries and colonizing activities," he wrote. He pointed out that he was a man of means with more resources at his disposal than any of the other people who had presented colonizing petitions. He reminded the king that there were millions of souls out there, waiting to be converted to Christianity, and he begged for the honor to be the one to make their conversion possible. The letter ends, "To his royal Catholic Majesty, from the humblest of his servants."

Soon afterward, Espejo sent his son-in-law to Spain as an emissary to speak directly to the king and sign the necessary contracts.

Then, to make certain that nothing went wrong, he decided to travel to Spain himself. But on the way, in Havana, Cuba, Espejo died.

# CHAPTER SIX

# Gaspar Castaño de Sosa

## He Leads a Fugitive Colony in Search of a Home

*In 1588, the viceroy — New Spain's*
*top government official — arrested the*
*founder and governor of the frontier state of*
*Nuevo León, just south of the present-day*
*Texas border, on charges of slaving.*
*That set the lieutenant governor,*
*Gaspar Castaño de Sosa, on a course*
*of illegal exploration and tragedy.*

——⊰•⊱——

I N THE DECADE SINCE NUEVO LEÓN HAD BEEN COLONIZED, MIN-ing was one of the few legitimate ways in which people with limited means could become wealthy — or just pro-vide a comfortable life for their families. Lured by the promise of rich silver mines, the settlers spent thousands of pesos and gambled everything they had to construct mills for smelting, grinding, and refining the ore. But the mines were so poor that what little silver the miners managed to extract didn't even pay for the charcoal used in smelting.

So, some turned to an illegal source of income: kidnapping Indians from remote areas and selling them farther south as slaves. The law considered the crime so heinous that the pun-ishment was death.

With the governor himself in prison and subject to exe-cution, many colonists decided to abandon the frontier and re-turn to the south. But Castaño de Sosa begged them to stay and proposed a radical solution: Head north, maybe to Quivira, and settle there.

Almost half a century had passed since Coronado reported that Quivira (in the general area of present-day Kansas) contained no wealth. The public imagination had transformed the area back into an idealized Promised Land.

The colonists agreed to go.

There was just one hitch. The Colonization Laws of 1573, designed to protect Indians, forbade colonization without permission of the king of Spain or the viceroy in New Spain. So, in the spring of 1590, Castaño de Sosa sent a message to the new viceroy requesting permission.

Castaño de Sosa didn't know that the outgoing viceroy had told the new one that the lieutenant governor and his men were "outlaws, criminals, and murderers" as heavily involved in the slave trade as the deposed governor.

The new viceroy replied to Castaño de Sosa's letter by ordering him to stop slaving at once. He also forbade the lieutenant governor to leave for New Mexico, as the whole, vaguely charted region north of present-day Mexico was still called.

Castaño de Sosa then sent messengers to tell the viceroy that he was going north to look for mines and that if he found any, he would establish a colony. He told his messengers that he would travel only as far north as the Río Grande and wait for 60 days. If the viceroy approved the plan, the messengers need not come.

On July 27, 1590, Castaño de Sosa set out with 170 men, women, and children. Enough carts accompanied them to carry a good six tons of equipment and supplies. That made the expedition the first known to travel with wheeled vehicles into what now is the American West. Castaño de Sosa appointed one of the wealthier colonists, Juan Pérez de los Ríos, as quartermaster and ordered him to ration the corn and wheat carefully.

As independent and stubborn as Castaño de Sosa himself, Pérez de los Ríos informed his boss that he would not make people subsist on short rations. Castaño de Sosa backed

**THIS SCULPTURE REPRESENTS THE SOLDIERS, CIVILIANS, AND PRIESTS WHO SETTLED NEW MEXICO.**

down. He had other things to worry about — wagons mired in rain-soaked ground, three natives who were stealing horses, and the abandonment of a wagon that broke down.

On September 9, the party reached the Río Grande, probably in the vicinity of present-day Del Rio, Texas.

Here, Castaño de Sosa hesitated. The viceroy was the supreme authority in New Spain: He represented the king. Never mind those murky arrangements Castaño de Sosa had made with his messengers. If he crossed these muddy waters, he would be subject to not just the viceroy's wrath, but also to the anger of Felipe II, king of Spain.

No wonder that at this point the wandering lieutenant governor grew weak, then ill.

While Castaño de Sosa recovered and waited for word from the viceroy, food supplies dwindled to only 100 fanegas of corn and wheat. That amount equaled a little more than four modern tons, but winter was coming, and the settlers had no idea where their next supplies would come from. Eating only one pound of food per person per day, they would devour everything on hand long before Christmas. Castaño de Sosa ordered Pérez de los Ríos to distribute the remaining rations, with each man, woman, and child allotted slightly more than one pound of grain a day.

The leader had decided by now to travel northwestward

to the Pueblo Indian country, rather than head straight north for Quivira. Too weak to go exploring himself, he sent Pérez de los Ríos to find the best route. Then he sent two more exploring parties. When they all returned, he held a council.

Castaño de Sosa himself wanted to follow the route explored by Pérez de los Ríos, but most of the men preferred another route. After much discussion, the men reluctantly agreed to follow Pérez de los Ríos's route.

Meanwhile, in Mexico City, the viceroy ordered one of Castaño de Sosa's enemies, Capt. Juan Morlete, to raise and equip an army of 40 top soldiers to find the runaway colonists.

"You will use every mild and prudent means you can to persuade them to give up their expedition and return with you," the viceroy ordered. Morlete was to confiscate their wagons and bring the prisoners and their possessions to Mexico City without delay.

That very day, October 1, 1590, unaware of the viceroy's command, Castaño de Sosa and the colonists plunged through the Río Grande and set foot in modern-day Texas.

Again and again, the rivers, ravines, and rocky terrain slowed the travelers, but the food shortage plagued them most. On October 14, Castaño de Sosa ordered rations cut in half, but Pérez de los Ríos donated some oxen as food. For a while that raised the daily ration to half a pound of grain and a pound and a half of meat per person. The travelers also roasted and ate agave plants.

The terrain grew worse. The wagon train passed through land so barren and dry, people feared they would die of thirst. Even Pérez de los Ríos urged Castaño de Sosa to turn back and find the road the other men had recommended. The possibility of losing all his capital and possessions confronted him, Pérez de los Ríos proclaimed, but threats to the safety of his wife and children far outweighed those concerns.

Faced with the opposition of his officers, Castaño de Sosa called the entire group together — men, women, children, and Indian servants — and pleaded with them to have faith that God would give him the wisdom to lead them out of the wilderness. He ordered them on, and they obeyed.

Sobbing now, Pérez de los Ríos begged Castaño de Sosa to turn back. Castaño de Sosa replied that anyone who showed fright would forfeit his rights as a colonist. To show his displeasure and his sense of rejection, he pulled away from the party and traveled alone.

In less than an hour, Castaño de Sosa found an enormous pool with enough water for animals and humans alike. The discovery proved to him that God had provided, and it unified the travelers.

But water shortages and other problems, large and small, persisted. Sometimes, the travelers stopped for only two hours at night so they could reach the next water hole sooner. Once, the thirst-crazed goats and oxen bolted off on their own search for water, but settlers rounded them up. The terrain was so rough that in one mountain chain the horses wore out 300 shoes. A little girl died. Wolves ate some goats. More wagons broke down. A tame deer belonging to a woman named Catalina de Charles broke its leg.

Finally, by the end of November, water became more plentiful and the terrain leveled out. As the weather grew colder, the band traveled northward through what is now eastern New Mexico, probably passing near present-day Roswell.

Few people complained openly now, but Castaño de Sosa spent more and more time exploring on his own. On December 3, he went off scouting for a better road and didn't return by dark. People lit signal fires to guide him home and berated themselves for letting him go off alone. Three men went searching, carrying lighted torches.

When they found him, safe and well, the settlers expressed gratitude and relief. Despite all the hardships and disagreements, they had bonded into a unit.

Two months had passed since the viceroy had ordered Morlete and his soldiers north after them, but hunger pursued the unsuspecting colonists far more relentlessly than Morlete.

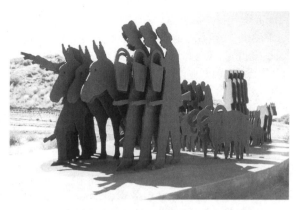

**CLOSER VIEW OF THE SCULPTURE**
*LA PUERTA DEL SOL* **(DOORWAY TO THE SUN).**

The only wheat that remained was seed they were saving to plant in their new homeland. So, they ate wild game, mesquite beans, and grass seed. When these sources of food failed them, Castaño de Sosa parceled out the seed wheat, until only 200 pounds remained.

From the reports of earlier travelers, he knew that Pueblo Indians lived nearby. Before Christmas, he sent scouts to search for them. He ordered the scouts not to enter the villages but to simply report back to him when they located them.

However, when the men reached Pecos Pueblo, some 20 miles east of present-day Santa Fe, the Indians welcomed them, offered them food, and urged them to come inside.

Cold and hungry, the scouts ignored Castaño de Sosa's order and accepted gratefully. For the first time in weeks, they slept soundly and warmly with full bellies. But in the morning, the Indians attacked them with bows, arrows, and stones. The outnumbered Spaniards fled, abandoning armor, weapons, saddles, and coats.

For days, the coatless men walked and rode bareback in bitter cold, wind, and snow. They grew so hungry, they ate a horse. When they finally reached the main party, they were greeted with great relief. Never mind that they had disobeyed orders. At least they were alive. Castaño de Sosa said he'd go to Pecos Pueblo, make peace, and retrieve their belongings.

Pérez de los Ríos donated three more oxen to supply the new expedition, and the day after Christmas, Castaño de Sosa left for Pecos, taking 20 soldiers and 20 servants.

In the bitter cold, stress levels soared.

One windy night, when a soldier tried to start a fire, a stray spark exploded a powder flask hanging from his belt, but he survived.

Then one of Castaño de Sosa's close friends, a black soldier named Pedro Flores, grew so depressed he wouldn't eat. Unable to sleep, he became incoherent. One night, while the others slept, Flores loaded his armor, harquebus, and other possessions onto his horse and disappeared. The settlers never saw him again.

On December 30, the soldiers made camp near Pecos Pueblo. The next morning, Castaño de Sosa ordered them to get up early and eat well: This was the day they would make peace with the Indians. He sent messengers to ask for peace. Then he and a few men rode forward in formation, with flag waving. The buglers blew trumpets.

The people of Pecos were at war with the Plains Indians. Already badly rattled, they found the white outsiders unnerving, particularly when Castaño de Sosa and five soldiers marched in formation around the village several times. At first the men and women of Pecos simply stood armed and ready on the upper terraces of the village. Then they shot arrows and threw rocks at the outsiders.

Twice more, the lieutenant governor tried to make peace, but failed.

About 2 o'clock that afternoon, the Spaniards attacked. Their harquebuses were more powerful than the Indian weapons, but the people of Pecos held firm until the Indian servants of the soldiers attacked with bows and arrows. Seeing their own weapons used against them disconcerted the Pecos warriors, and the battle soon ended.

Cautiously, on New Year's Day, 1591, the Indians made peace with the explorers, who now roamed through the town. Never before had they seen an earthen village of its type, and they found it fascinating. The village's 16 kivas especially impressed the shivering travelers. The underground chambers were so well designed that they kept people warm all winter, heated only by braziers banked with ashes. The visitors also marveled at the large quantities of corn supplies, which they estimated at 30,000 fanegas — about 3 million pounds. Hungrily, they noted that the Indians also stored chile peppers, herbs, beans, and squash in their homes.

Sending 22 fanegas of food back to the other colonists, Castaño de Sosa decided to investigate mining possibilities. When he and his remaining men passed through the site of present-day Santa Fe, they had to break ice on the Santa Fe River to reach drinking water. Continuing north, they traveled from village to village. Everywhere Castaño de Sosa went, he showed people mineral samples he had brought from Mexico and asked where he could find more. Often, the Indians said they'd seen similar rocks nearby. But he could never find them.

The villagers gave the outsiders firewood and fed them corn, flour, beans, squashes, tortillas, and turkeys. But the Indians of San Juan Pueblo were not happy to see them. Still, a few came out into the three feet of snow on the ground and gave the ritual greeting: blowing their breath on their hands, then placing their hands on Castaño de Sosa's face. In turn, he kissed their hands.

Meanwhile, still camped several days east of Pecos Pueblo, the main party of colonists ate the last kernel of corn and waited numbly for their leader. When he returned, late in January, they followed him back toward the Río Grande to continue searching for mines. They still had no inkling that they were being pursued by an army from Mexico City, but they had grown so frazzled, they probably would not have cared.

Near the Cerrillos Mountains, east of the Río Grande at a village they named San Marcos, they discovered a vein of silver ore. But as hard as they tried, they couldn't extract the silver.

Tensions grew. When Castaño de Sosa dragged the colonists off in search of another rumored mine, they protested. Some wanted to return to New Spain. Others resented their leader because he refused to let them plunder the natives' possessions and food.

Oblivious to their resentment, Castaño de Sosa made plans to send a party of soldiers back to Mexico to recruit more colonists. He appointed a soldier named Alonso Jaimez to lead the proposed expedition.

Meanwhile, he started moving the base camp from San Marcos to Santo Domingo Pueblo, along the Río Grande.

Half a dozen soldiers decided that the only way to stop this mad wandering was to kill Castaño de Sosa. Before they could act, he heard of the plot.

It appeared that the ringleader was Alonso Jaimez. Enraged, Castaño de Sosa ordered loyal soldiers to strangle Jaimez.

For seven months the bedraggled colonists had endured one calamity after the other. Now the thought that one of their own would be executed was too much. Men and women alike rushed forward and begged Castaño de Sosa to pardon Jaimez and his accomplices.

Their pleas so touched Castaño de Sosa that he suspended the death sentence and pardoned Jaimez's accomplices. In an act of true charity, he even struck their names from the record, so that no one outside the group would ever know the traitors' identity.

Soon afterward, on March 11, another group of settlers begged Castaño de Sosa for permission to return to New Spain.

Discouraged, the lieutenant governor-turned-explorer told the settlers that they could leave. He would rather stay and die among the Indians than be the cause of more problems, he said.

These words so touched his fellow explorers that they changed their minds and stayed.

Once again, the travelers felt united, ready to follow their leader until they found the right place to settle down.

But a few days later, while Castaño de Sosa was exploring south of Santo Domingo, Captain Morlete arrived at Santo Domingo Pueblo with his soldiers.

Given the news, Castaño de Sosa galloped back to Santo Domingo. As he approached the village, friends rushed out and begged him not to enter because the soldiers were going to arrest him.

Castaño de Sosa told them that he had done nothing wrong. "But if it is the king's will to have me arrested, I will gladly submit."

Calmly, he presented himself to Captain Morlete. The two leaders and their men exchanged embraces. Then Morlete arrested Castaño de Sosa. The long-time adventurer stood quietly and allowed Captain Morlete's men to shackle him.

Despite orders to return straight to Mexico, Morlete lingered among the Indian settlements of the Río Grande. By July 10, he and his prisoners had gone no further south than the site of present-day Las Cruces.

All the way to Mexico City, Castaño de Sosa remained in leg irons and chains. On July 27, exactly a year after he had led the settlers north, the broken leader wrote to the viceroy from the road. Captivity had destroyed his health, he said, and he felt shame and "grievous sorrow."

Alluding to the accusation of slave trading, Castaño de Sosa denied that he ever had engaged in it. He begged the viceroy to put things in perspective and said, "It seemed to me that in this recent journey I had rendered a service important to God and the king, as I firmly believe it will some day prove to be."

In Mexico City, the viceroy imprisoned Castaño de Sosa. By February 1592, he was on trial in that city before the highest court in New Spain, the Audencia. One year later, on February 13, 1593, the Audencia passed sentence.

The sentencing document listed these crimes: raising

troops without authorization; invading lands inhabited by peaceful Indians; and going to New Mexico. But it did not charge him with slaving.

The Audencia sentenced the illegal explorer to "exactly six years of exile from the jurisdiction of New Spain." It ordered him to live in the Philippines and work, with pay, as a civil servant. The sentence carried with it a clause that it could not be appealed. Nonetheless, Castaño de Sosa's supporters took his case to a higher court: the Council of the Indies in Spain.

Meanwhile, in the Philippines, Castaño de Sosa's spirit of adventure and his years of frontier living apparently helped him adjust to his new life. He made friends.

In Spain, the Council of the Indies found Castaño de Sosa innocent on all counts. He could return to New Spain and resume his life.

The news never reached him. Times were as troubled in the Philippines as on New Spain's northern frontier. One source of turbulence: Chinese men had been kidnapped from their homeland and forced to work as slaves.

While Castaño de Sosa was sailing to the Mollucas Islands, in present-day Indonesia, the ship's Chinese galley slaves revolted. Those they killed included Castaño de Sosa.

# CHAPTER SEVEN

# Murder on the Trail
## Two Renegade Soldiers
## March Into Disaster

*Rumors of fabulous wealth and glorious
adventures in the north didn't die with
Gaspar Castaño de Sosa's problem-filled
expedition and arrest for illegal exploration.
Other would-be explorers and colonizers
simply imagined that they would
be more successful than he. Some wanted
the adventure. Some wanted the gold.*

———◦———

ABOUT THE TIME THE CITIZENS OF MEXICO CITY WERE TALK-
ing about Gaspar Castaño de Sosa's misfortunes and
trial, Antonio Gutiérrez de Humaña arrived in the capital. A soldier-settler from the frontier state of Nueva Vizcaya
(present-day Durango and Chihuahua), he may have been on
business for the governor. But he also had private business,
during which he met Jusepe, an Indian who was looking for
work as a servant.

"I'm planning an expedition into the north," he told
Jusepe. "Are you willing to join me?"

Jusepe may not have known about the law that forbade
unauthorized exploring and colonizing. But if he did, he knew
that the law wouldn't bother to punish servants. He took the job
and followed his new employer back to Nueva Vizcaya. There
he met Gutiérrez de Humaña's friend and fellow officer,
Francisco Leyva de Bonilla.

Without permission or authorization, the two men were

talking among the soldier-settlers of Nueva Vizcaya, looking for people who would like to accompany them north to the Río Grande, into Pueblo Indian country, and perhaps beyond.

While the two officers waited for the right moment to head north without attracting attention, they continued their work as soldiers.

As lawmen would three centuries later, soldiers on the northern frontier of New Spain dealt with such problems as rustlers and Indians who refused to adapt to European ways. In 1593, cattle thieves were harassing the settlers of Nueva Vizcaya. The governor believed the rustlers were unfriendly Indians who were hiding out along the northern frontier.

It was one thing to protect Indians from Spanish colonists, as the law required, and quite another to allow Indians to get away with stealing Spanish cattle. The governor decided to send a party of soldiers to chase and punish the rustlers.

The man he selected to lead the party was Captain Leyva de Bonilla.

The moment had come. The chase would be their cover. Leyva de Bonilla invited Gutiérrez de Humaña and the other soldier-settlers who had agreed to go north to participate in the chase. Jusepe and other servants helped them get their families and a few possessions ready, and they all charged northward.

Learning what his soldiers were up to infuriated the governor. He sent a messenger with orders that they return or face charges of treason. Some obeyed. But approximately 30 soldiers continued northward with Leyva de Bonilla and Gutiérrez de Humaña.

One or both men must have carefully chronicled their journey. Unfortunately, those records didn't survive, and we do not know today how many women, servants, and children accompanied the soldiers. It is known that Jusepe was only one of many Mexican servants who stayed with them as they headed north. A soldier named Sánchez brought his little son, Alonso. One woman, perhaps a servant, perhaps a wife, was half Spanish and half African, but her name has not survived.

The governor informed the viceroy of Leyva de Bonilla and Gutiérrez de Humaña's treachery, but the viceroy had other worries and put the problem off.

Meanwhile, the renegades reached San Ildefonso Pueblo, along the upper Río Grande. The inhabitants were friendly, and the Spaniards decided to settle down. For about a year, they lived among these Tewa-speaking Indians, making short explorations into the surrounding countryside to visit other Pueblo villages.

Then something disrupted the settler-renegades; it isn't clear what. Both leaders were said to have a fondness for native women; if so, that would have made the Pueblo Indians lose patience with them quickly. Barring that, the Indians of San Ildefonso may simply have grown tired of their long-term guests, who almost certainly treated them like servants. Or maybe the settlers heard someone repeat el Turco's old tale, that a civilized and fabulously wealth country lay somewhere to the northeast, out in the great buffalo plains.

Whatever the cause, Leyva de Bonilla and Gutiérrez de Humaña packed up the entire party — men, women, children, and servants — and headed eastward. Traveling slowly, they stopped and set up tents each night. It took a full month to reach the buffalo. They angled northward and traveled another 15 days, until they arrived at two large rivers. On the other side, they found numerous Indian villages. Beyond these lay the fabled Quivira (probably in present-day Kansas).

In Coronado's day, Quivira had consisted of 25 separate settlements. But in the last 50 years, these had merged into one vast city. It took the explorers two days to travel from one end to the other. They estimated it to be almost 30 miles long and nearly six miles wide — stretching nearly 200 square miles across a flat plain. About 200,000 people lived there, making the city a true metropolis, larger by far than any other native settlement the travelers had seen.

But like Coronado before them, Leyva de Bonilla and Gutiérrez de Humaña discovered that Quivira contained no silver,

**THE QUIVIRANS COULD OFFER FOOD,
BUT NO GOLD.**

no gold. The city abounded only in food, houses, people, and kindness. The Quivirans welcomed their guests and gave them "abundant supplies of food."

Even lacking silver and gold, Quivira fascinated the two explorers and their followers.

To build a house, the inhabitants constructed a frame of poles and covered it with straw. They placed dwellings close together, facing narrow streets, or paths. One of the rivers the soldiers had crossed earlier flowed through Quivira, providing water not just for people, but for crops. At intervals, city planners had left open spaces between the houses for people to grow corn, beans, and squash. Mostly, though, buffalo fueled the local economy, providing inhabitants with food and many of the tools and furnishings of daily life.

Until now, Leyva de Bonilla and Gutiérrez de Humaña seem to have gotten along well as joint leaders of the illegal expedition. But tensions must have risen sometimes, perhaps over women, perhaps over what course to follow next. In Quivira something unraveled whatever unity of purpose had existed between the two outlaw officers.

It is easy to imagine that one leader wanted to go back, either to San Ildefonso or to Nueva Vizcaya, while the other wanted to press on. Or perhaps one leader blamed the other for what may have seemed like a wasted and futile trip. Or maybe one wanted adventure, and the other wanted gold.

Jusepe watched and listened as the explorers absorbed a new rumor they heard at Quivira: Farther on lay settlements even larger than this. Not just cities, but gold.

As the travelers headed northward from Quivira, the two leaders argued openly. One day Leyva de Bonilla threatened to beat Gutiérrez de Humaña severely with a stick.

The party was passing through completely unfamiliar territory now. Jusepe and the other travelers grew increasingly tense.

At a place where the land was so flat that the travelers could see no mountains or hills, an enormous buffalo herd completely covered the plain. When the explorers reached the other side of the herd, the travelers could find no more Indian settlements.

On the 10th day after leaving Quivira, they encountered a deep, sluggish river almost three quarters of a mile wide. This may have been the Platte River of Nebraska or even the Missouri River, where it forms Nebraska's northeastern boundary with South Dakota.

The explorers did not dare to cross the river, so they made camp.

All afternoon, Gutíerrez de Humaña stayed in his tent, writing. The next morning, he continued filling page after page with words. Then he sent a soldier, Miguel Pérez, to call Captain Leyva de Bonilla.

Dressed only in shirt and breeches, Levya de Bonilla approached his fellow officer and former friend's tent.

Whatever Leyva de Bonilla might have been expecting, it surely wasn't what he got.

Gutiérrez de Humaña came out to meet him. When they were so close to each other that they could have shaken hands, Gutiérrez de Humaña pulled a large knife from his pocket. Before Leyva de Bonilla could back away, or onlookers intervene, Gutiérrez de Humaña stabbed Leyva de Bonilla twice.

The captain died, and the soldiers buried him hastily, as if to blot out what had happened.

Jusepe, thoroughly jangled by now, stayed just long enough to observe Gutiérrez de Humaña showing some papers to the other soldiers. Then Jusepe and four other Mexican Indian servants slipped quietly away from the camp and started on the long journey back toward the Pueblo country of the Río Grande.

For days they traveled together in a southwesterly direction across the plains. But one day they got separated. Three men disappeared, and Jusepe and his remaining companion never saw them again.

As the two men journeyed toward the Pueblos, they came to a village of Plains Indians, perhaps Comanches. Always before, traveling with the Spaniards, the Mexican servants had been safe as they visited this village and that. But now their protectors weren't with them. The inhabitants killed Jusepe's friend, and he fled on alone.

Apaches captured him and made him a slave. For a year he worked for them before he could escape.

Six years had elapsed since Jusepe left Mexico City in the employ of Gutiérrez de Humaña; it was now the summer of 1598. When Jusepe reached a village near Pecos Pueblo, he heard that more Spaniards were staying at San Juan Pueblo. He traveled to the pueblo, where don Juan de Oñate and the first legal Spanish colonists had just arrived. Jusepe attached himself to the new settlement and once again began working as a servant.

All this time, back in New Spain, no word had ever been received regarding Leyva de Bonilla and Gutiérrez de Humaña and their companions. From the viceroy on down, people believed the runaway soldiers and their families had settled down happily, somewhere in the north. Part of Oñate's duties as the first legal colonizer of the north country was to track down the illegal explorers, arrest them, and send them home.

But when Jusepe first appeared at San Juan Pueblo, Oñate was so new to the area and so busy with other projects and problems that he paid little attention to the wandering Mexican Indian. Finally, six months later, Jusepe gave a report of his experiences to Oñate, who forwarded it to the viceroy. But even Jusepe didn't know what had happened to Gutiérrez de Humaña and the other travelers after the murder. Based on Jusepe's report, Oñate and the viceroy concluded that the surviving renegade and his companions must still be living among the Indians of Quivira, or beyond.

In 1601, Oñate took Jusepe and 70 soldiers and headed for Quivira. When they reached the vicinity of present-day Kansas, they began to hear fragments of stories about Gutiérrez de Humaña. Every narrator placed the location differently, but all agreed that somewhere, perhaps as much as 18 days from Quivira, Indians had attacked Gutiérrez de Humaña and the settlers.

Using fire as their weapon, the attackers created a circle of flames that devoured the vagabonds. Gutiérrez de Humaña and the others, who in the public's imagination had been living so happily and carefree, died a terrible death.

Only two people survived. One was Alonso, the little son of the soldier named Sánchez. The other was the half-African woman. She had been burned badly in the fire.

Some Indians told Oñate that this woman had healed and was living among other Indians three days farther on.

Before Oñate and his men could reach her, or hunt for young Alonso Sánchez, 1,500 Indians formed a semi-circle around the Spaniards and attacked. Arrows thickened the air, and the Spaniards barely escaped the fate of Gutiérrez de Humaña, or of Fray Juan Padilla 60 years earlier. Virtually every Spaniard in the party was wounded, but by some miracle, none seriously. Oñate decided it was foolish to risk his men's lives by searching for Gutiérrez de Humaña's two survivors. They returned to Pueblo country.

Nothing more was heard of the woman, but later it was said that Alonso Sánchez grew up among the Indians, without ever seeing another Spaniard. As a young man, he developed a reputation for such fierceness and courage that he became a great leader, both respected and feared by the Indians who had raised him.

Meanwhile, back in New Spain, the myth circulated again that Quivira overflowed with gold. It was said that the Indians mined the precious metal in seven hills set on a plain. It was said that Gutiérrez de Humaña and his companions had died while returning to New Spain "loaded with gold."

# CHAPTER EIGHT

# The First Roundup
### Soldiers Saddle Up to Become Buffalo Ranchers

*Deep in New Spain, early Spanish explorers
saw their first buffalo in Montezuma's zoo.
After that, the great, shaggy beast, whose
natural range at that time probably didn't
extend south of the present U.S.-Mexican border,
fascinated the Spanish almost as much as
Spanish horses fascinated the Indians.
As settlers moved north, they dreamed of
owning huge buffalo herds.*

———❦———

**M**ANY OF THE FIRST SOLDIER-COLONISTS WHO ARRIVED
with don Juan de Oñate in northern New Mexico in
July 1598 barely had time to unpack. On September
16, Oñate sent his young nephew, Vicente de Zaldívar Mendoza,
and nearly half his soldiers out onto the plains to search for an
exotic animal, the hump-backed *cíbola*, as the Spanish called the
buffalo.

Alvar Nuñez Cabeza de Vaca, who saw the huge animals
only three times in his travels, described the meat as being
finer and fatter than European cattle. Coronado called buffalo
"very wild and ferocious." One of Coronado's explorers labeled
them "the most monstrous thing in the way of animals which
has ever been seen or read about."

Given that kind of reputation, it's not surprising that the
first expedition the colonists undertook, once the carts had
arrived and the church was in place, was to search for buffalo.

Zaldívar's soldiers had a second mission, too, to find and arrest outlaw explorers Francisco Leyva de Bonilla and Antonio Gutiérrez de Humaña and their followers. For a guide and interpreter, Zaldívar brought Jusepe, the Mexican Indian who had accompanied Leyva de Bonilla and Gutiérrez de Humaña all the way to Quivira. But at this point, Jusepe had still not revealed his story, probably because no one had asked.

Zaldívar, only 25, was medium-sized with a reddish brown beard and a good sense of direction. He took 60 soldiers and headed eastward, well-supplied with food and spare horses.

The men were in a good mood. After so many months of slow, measured movement with the caravan of settlers, they were traveling fast, light, and free. The people they encountered seemed pleasant and well fed. The land itself appeared bountiful. One night, camped on the Gallinas River near present-day Las Vegas, New Mexico, they threw in their fishing lines and caught more than 500 catfish, pulling in 1,000 pounds of fish within three hours.

As they headed north along the eastern side of the Sangre de Cristo Mountains, toward the grazing grounds of the buffalo, they tried to picture where the shipwrecked Cabeza de Vaca had traveled in relation to where they were now. They mingled with local Indians and commented on the women's shoes and buckskin trousers. Most men went naked; only a few wore buffalo robes or blankets.

Above all, Zaldívar and his men talked about the fabulous animals that had lured them eastward. Based on what they had heard, they decided they wouldn't be satisfied until each man had 10,000 head of buffalo in his own corral.

Farther east, Coronado had traveled through thick buffalo herds for days, but here, on the western edge of the Great Plains, Zaldívar had to work hard to find them.

When the men finally saw their first buffalo, they considered the sighting hilarious, in light of their dreams: An old, solitary bull wandered alone.

Farther on, however, they found 300 buffalo drinking at

some pools. About 18 miles beyond that, they encountered another thousand head.

Immediately, they began to construct a corral. But the buffalo, sensing trouble, moved on, and construction ceased.

An Indian guide told the Spaniards that the animals grazed in great numbers along the Canadian River, where it flowed down from the Sangres. Zaldívar left the main party behind and led 10 soldiers north. They'd almost reached the buffalo herd, when a trading party of Plains Indians scared the animals away.

If Zaldívar was disappointed, he didn't say so. Instead, he focused his attention and curiosity on the members of the trading party and other natives he met. From Taos, the traders brought corn, cotton blankets, pottery, and turquoise, which they had purchased with salt and the hides, meat, tallow, and suet of buffalo.

Heading back to the main party, Zaldívar passed through an Indian encampment of 50 teepees shaped like bells and made of tanned buffalo hides. Bright red and white, the tents were "built as skillfully as those of Italy and so large that in the most ordinary ones four different mattresses and beds were easily accommodated," he wrote. The leather was so well tanned that no matter how hard it rained, no water passed through it. When the hides dried, they remained soft and pliable.

Enchanted, Zaldívar bought one to take back to San Juan. Even the weight astonished him: only 50 pounds.

The Indians' use of dogs as pack animals also fascinated him. "They drive great trains of them," he wrote. Each dog dragged a 100-pound burden on poles that trailed behind it. The women loaded the dogs, holding them steady by grasping the animals' heads between their knees.

As Zaldívar traveled farther eastward, reunited with his men, Jusepe pointed out two of Leyva de Bonilla and Gutiérrez de Humaña's old campsites, about 30 miles apart. Horse dung and charcoal from the campfires still lay around. Apparently, Zaldívar still failed to question Jusepe about the missing men.

**AN EARLY SPANISH PORTRAIT
OF THE AMERICAN BUFFALO.**

Rather than picturing the outlaw explorers' slow trip across the plains, Zaldívar imagined them fleeing soldiers.

Near the old campsites, Zaldívar encountered a buffalo herd so vast, he estimated it at 100,000 head. At once the men began building a corral large enough to hold 10,000 animals. This time the buffalo continued grazing as the men piled up large cottonwood logs to create great wings that would funnel the animals into the main enclosure.

They finished in three backbreaking days. Then they rode out to the herd. Charging among the animals, the horsemen herded them toward the corral. Now alerted, however, the buffalo began stampeding. Galloping among the frantic animals, the horsemen herded the speeding beasts toward the corral.

Just when it seemed the roundup was succeeding, the buffalo herd swung around and stampeded in the opposite direction.

Hollering and galloping among them, the men tried to herd them back toward the corral, but the buffalo pounded onward. When a horse got in their way, they gored it and continued their pell-mell flight. Zaldívar and his men couldn't catch the fleeing bison. It seemed as if the thundering animals actually knew what their pursuers were doing: When the soldiers stopped, the buffalo stopped, too. They lay in the dirt and rolled around like mules. Then they continued on.

As Zaldívar put it, "It was impossible to stop them, because they are terribly obstinate cattle, courageous beyond exaggeration, and so cunning."

For the next several days, Zaldívar and his men tried "a thousand ways" to surround the buffalo or to shut them into the corral. Still, the buffalo refused to be captured. Watching them, Zaldívar concluded that the animals didn't fear people, because again and again they responded to the futile herding by attacking the Spaniards' horses.

Lowering their heads, they charged forward, thrusting their long horns into the horses' sides. Before the Spaniards gave up, the buffalo had killed three horses and badly wounded 40 more. "Remarkably savage," Zaldívar called the bison.

Outmaneuvered, the Spaniards collected 1,000 pounds of tallow from dead buffalo to take back to San Juan. Then they made one final try. If they couldn't corral adult animals, they could at least start their own herds by capturing some calves.

However, even the youngest animals refused to give up their freedom. Some died struggling to escape the ropes that pulled them along behind the horses. Others, strapped down on the horses' backs, died from shock or fright. Either way, all the calves died within an hour of being captured.

Through all this, Zaldívar found himself admiring the mighty buffalo more and more. "The more one sees [the buffalo], the more one desires to see it," he wrote. "No one could be so melancholy that if he were to see it a hundred times a day, he could keep from laughing heartily as many times, or could fail to marvel at the sight of so ferocious an animal."

Meanwhile, November came, and with it, winter. The men hadn't reached Quivira, and they still knew nothing more about

Leyva de Bonilla and Gutiérrez de Humaña's fate, but it was time to head home.

Wiser in the ways of the buffalo, the 61 men rode slowly back to San Juan Pueblo, leading their injured horses. They didn't have a single live buffalo to show for their 54-day adventure.

Still the men couldn't completely give up their dream of owning vast herds of buffalo. As he rode, Zaldívar made plans. If the men returned during calving season and captured newborn calves, they could give the calves over to the care of domestic cows and goats, whose example would tame them. Or perhaps these wild cattle, as he still considered them, could be bred with domestic cattle and be tamed.

It was not to be. But the expedition did yield the first real news of Leyva de Bonilla and Gutiérrez de Humaña. In the middle of a hectic and difficult winter, Oñate finally took time to question Jusepe and forward his report to the viceroy.

Meanwhile, Vicente de Zaldívar wrote his own report on the West's first roundup. Four centuries later, it remains a splendid tribute to the beauty, poetry, and power of the West's native "cattle."

# CHAPTER NINE

# Settling In
## Outside, Under, Around, and Above the Law

*Two and a half centuries before the rowdy days
of the United States' Wild West, some frontier
folk lived bawdy, tempestuous lives in New
Spain's northern region. At least, reports of
their activities contain such references.*

━━◆◆◆━━

ROUND 1605, SETTLERS BEGAN FARMING IN WHAT IS NOW
the Santa Fe area, and by 1610 the colonists had moved
the capital of Nuevo México to Santa Fe. There they
settled into an isolated but colorful lifestyle. Despite the presence of the Church and officials of the king, the unruly colonists
lived by their own rules. The details that have survived come
mainly from reports sent back to Mexico by friars and politicians, who always were engaged in a fierce power struggle.

Spaniards themselves sometimes propagated the stereo-
types of the *leyenda negra,* the Black Legend that considered all
things Spanish evil. Fray Jerónimo de Zárate Salmerón, a
Franciscan friar who was born into a Spanish family in Mexico
about 1560, said that the typical Spaniard was so hungry for silver and gold that he would "enter Hell itself to obtain them," but
that the settlers were "enemies of all kinds of work." The friar,
who lived in New Mexico between about 1618 and 1626, said
of the settlers, "As long as they have a good supply of tobacco
to smoke, they are very contented, and they do not want any
more riches . . ."

To illustrate his point, the scandalized Franciscan told
the story of three men from Flanders, living in Mexico City,

who traveled to New Mexico in 1618. In Santa Fe, they found an unused workshop an optimistic governor, don Pedro de Peralta, had built for processing ore. In the surrounding countryside, the Flemings found a number of potential silver mines and did assays to determine the richness of the ore. Then they returned to New Spain to buy mining equipment. They hired a miner and a refiner, and started back to New Mexico.

The news that the Flemings were returning, ready to mine and process silver, reached northern New Mexico shortly ahead of them. That very night, arsonists burned down Peralta's workshop. To Fray Zárate Salmerón, that proved that New Mexicans were "enemies of silver and do not want anyone else to mine it."

New Mexicans saw themselves — and the friars — in a different light. In a 1617 letter, Santa Fe city official Francisco Pérez Granillo wrote apologetically to the authorities in Mexico: "Señores, the people of this New Mexico have little learning." Writing to the viceroy in February 1639, members of the town council reported, "the inhabitants are few, poor, and have little knowledge of business affairs or of anything except arms, while the friars are many and enjoy rich profits, acquired from the labor of the natives and the poverty of the Spaniards." At one point, a New Mexican even accused a friar named Pedro de Escobar of having been a highwayman before becoming a friar.

Other accusations flew back and forth. The friars accused one governor of being a rustler, saying he had stolen 800 cows, 400 mares, and "a large number of sheep," and sent them south to Nueva Vizcaya.

Some friars acted as lawlessly as those they accused. In 1613, Fray Luís de Tirado ordered the citizens of Santa Fe to kill Governor Peralta, even though he had committed no crime. When the citizens refused, Fray Isidro Ordóñez kidnapped the governor and imprisoned him at the convent in Sandia Pueblo. The high-handed friar illegally prevented Governor Peralta from carrying out his duties as governor and even imprisoned other people who tried to notify the viceroy of the friars' crimes.

Nine months later, Peralta escaped from his convent

prison. Covered only with a buffalo robe, the emaciated governor walked half naked through the snow to a farm six miles away. His jailer, Fray Esteban de Perea, reportedly raised an army of Indians, armed with bows and arrows, and surrounded the farm, but Governor Peralta made it back to Santa Fe, exhausted and starving.

On Ordoñez's orders, the friars captured the governor again, put him in leg irons, and seated him on a horse "like a woman." In bitter cold, with wind and blowing snow, they escorted him back to prison

Eventually Peralta returned safely to New Spain, where the scant surviving records suggest the courts vindicated him.

But for the citizens of Nuevo México and the more sensible friars, the early decades of the 1600s remained a time of "muchos terrores" — many terrors. Francisco Pérez Granillo, the municipal official from Santa Fe, said that Ordoñez and Tirado had taken advantage of their ignorance. "We now find ourselves called traitors, some of us suffering imprisonment, some have fled, and others are about to lose their property, honor, and life."

One friar, Andrés Juárez, became so agitated that he threatened to kill either himself or Ordóñez. Another friar, old and in poor health, grew so upset with Ordoñez's bullying that he got into a fist fight with the younger friar.

Given that kind of free-for-all atmosphere, in which people of all backgrounds considered themselves above the law, it's no wonder that another governor, Juan de Eulate, reportedly threatened to execute friars. They, in turn, accused him of heresy, immorality, slave trading, protecting Indian sorcerers, and other crimes.

In 1627, the next governor, Felipe Sotelo Osorio, had something of a more swashbuckling reputation. One winter evening in 1627, the governor and some soldiers were sitting around a candle-lit gambling table playing cards when the governor and a soldier started arguing.

"You'd better watch out. I've fought with some of the

**TRAINED AS MEN-AT-ARMS, MANY COLONISTS WERE HANDY WITH SWORD AND HARQUEBUS.**

bravest men in Spain — and won," the governor said. "If I had to, I'd fight with St. Peter and St. Paul themselves."

The soldier continued to goad the governor.

With an oath, the governor leapt up and started to pull his sword, then thought better of it, kicked over the candles and the gambling table, and stormed out.

But nothing quite matches the story of two socially elite Santa Fe women, a widowed mother and her married daughter, who kept the town gossiping intermittently for months on end between 1626 and 1631. The mother, Beatriz de los Angeles, a native of New Spain, knew how to make herbal remedies, aphrodisiacs, and other love potions. So did her daughter, Juana de la Cruz. Some brews included such everyday ingredients as corn and milk. Others contained fried worms, urine, or human excrement.

If the record is even close to accurate, it was common in the early 1600s in Santa Fe for wives to have lovers and husbands to have mistresses. Women sometimes came to Beatriz and Juana to buy potions to make men desire them.

All this was apparently so routine that no record of either woman would have survived except that both Beatriz and Juana were said to have used such potions — and worse — themselves, with scandalous results.

Beatriz had a lover, Diego Bellido. They quarreled. He beat her. They quarreled again. One day, Beatriz mixed herbs into a glass of milk or *atole* — a corn-meal drink — and gave it to her troublesome lover.

Soon afterward, Diego became violently ill with intestinal pains. Days later, he died.

There was no way to prove that Beatriz had killed Diego, but the more people talked, the more the story — and Beatriz's alleged guilt — grew. Soon, it was said that before she killed Diego, she'd tested her brew on two Indian servants, both of whom died.

Then it was said that it wasn't poisoned *atole* that killed Diego and the servants. It was a hex. In fact, another servant reported seeing Beatriz bury idols representing Diego and another person inside her hearth. Frantically, the servant tried to dig up the idols to save lives. But she couldn't find the idol that represented Diego, so he had died.

From there the story grew and spread, until it reached the friars.

Meanwhile, it was said that Juana had killed her own lover, for similar reasons and in similar ways. This story, too, mushroomed. People said that Juana had the evil eye and that she had killed a child just by touching it. They said that she had many lovers and that she could change into a glowing orb and fly through the sky at night, to visit each one and make sure he remained faithful to her.

Juana's story too reached the friars, including Fray Esteban de Perea, Peralta's former jailer, who by now had become the agent of the Inquisition in New Mexico. But the jaded friar had been in New Mexico a long time, and the gossip about Juana and Beatriz seemed trivial compared to the upheavals he had witnessed years earlier as Governor Peralta's jailer. He seems to

**THE FRIARS HAD A DISMAL VIEW
OF THE COLONISTS' HONESTY.**

have reasoned that, after all, the women hadn't blasphemed the Trinity, the saints, or the friars. They hadn't fought with the friars over questions of control.

Perea concluded that whatever the women had done, it was hardly heresy. Besides, he pointed out, the women who made all these wild charges included Juana's sisters-in-law, who were, in the friar's estimation, as guilty of immorality as Juana and Beatriz.

Behavior labeled immoral did in fact bring people to trial by the Inquisition. But Perea dismissed the case and wrote to his superiors in New Spain that it was hard to grow excited about a few herbs and powders. He did, however, moan that it seemed impossible for the colonists, who grew up "without discipline and schools," to distinguish the truth from lies. Even the most honorable among them lied as readily as they told the truth, he claimed. Part of the problem, he believed, was that too many foreigners lived in New Mexico.

Eventually, public attention shifted away from the women and back to the conflict between citizens and friars. Santa Feans sent furious complaints about the friars to New Spain. Friars were buying oxen for 14 pesos a piece and charging the king 40 pesos each, the complaints said. Friars were burning down the farms of Spanish settlers. Friars were attacking the governors and justices, thereby "terrorizing private persons and poor people."

Worst of all, as they had been for two decades, the friars were excommunicating people right and left and "denying confession to this entire community."

Is it any wonder?

# The German and the Inquisition

## The Immigrant Relies on His Mysterious Charms

*Heresy seems like an absurd charge today. However, after Spain's long and difficult battle to reclaim its land from Arabian Muslims, or the Moors as the Spanish called them, both the Church and the Crown saw heresy as a serious crime, on par with treason. It was punishable by death, and being a German citizen on the remote edges of the frontier was no protection.*

━━◈━━

I<small>N</small> 1569, <small>THE KING OF</small> S<small>PAIN ORDERED A TRIBUNAL OF THE</small> Inquisition set up in Mexico City. Called the Holy Office or Holy Tribunal, it had nearly unlimited powers, and even people who lived on the far northern frontiers of New Spain sometimes suffered terribly at the Inquisition's hand. Like a fair number of other frontier residents, agents of the Inquisition sometimes ignored the viceroy and even defied the king.

Legally, every Christian was obligated to report anyone whose action or words seemed subversive of the Christian faith in any way. New converts — Indians, for instance — were exempt from the Inquisition, but foreigners weren't. Accusations were sometimes incredibly petty. In a frontier case in 1670, the defendant was accused of swearing all day long and of saying, "I'm poorer than the devil."

Still, many settlers in what is now the West acted

remarkably unconcerned about the risks of trouble with the Inquisition. In the 1600s they remained as independent and stubborn as those who had gone before them.

The settlers ignored more mundane dangers, too. They refused to let the brutally cold winters, the inferno-like summers, or the hazardous travel slow them down. Even after they'd found a farm or community in which to settle down, they sometimes traveled hundreds or thousands of miles, usually on horseback, but occasionally on foot.

Werner Gruber was even more mobile — and more incautious about the Inquisition — than most.

Gruber, who was German, was born into a Catholic family in Germany during the 30 Years' War, a destructive series of religious and political conflicts that produced turmoil, social upheaval, and disease throughout large swaths of Europe. Hardships he had seen or endured as a child may have helped prepare him for the difficult life of a frontiersman in northern New Spain. In any case, by the mid-1600s, Gruber had left Germany and resettled in New Spain.

By the 1660s, he was living in the mining district of Sonora, south of present-day Arizona, where people knew him as Bernardo de Uber, Bernardo de Uberque, or simply, el Alemán — the German.

Overall, Gruber seems to have gotten along well in Sonora. Although he could not read and could write only a few words, by the time he reached Sonora, he spoke Spanish fluently. With a natural talent for buying and selling, he soon established himself as a successful merchant.

Gruber's neighbors in Sonora may have considered him superstitious. He made no secret of his belief in the power of incantations and charms, which, although he surely didn't know it, were an outgrowth of ancient German folk traditions. A Jesuit who worked in the mining district — quite likely a German himself — warned his fellow immigrant that superstitions were evil and the work of the devil, but Gruber ignored him and concentrated on making a living.

Using Sonora as his home base, Gruber took his merchandise on the road, journeying well over a thousand miles on a typical buying and selling trip along his customary route. He traveled north into what is now Arizona. At that time, no Spanish colonists lived there, but he brought trade goods to the Apaches and other Indians. From Arizona, he traveled eastward to the Spanish settlements and mission communities, where he sold what one contemporary called "merchandise and other trifles which this kingdom lacks."

Gruber's operation constituted a sort of one-man mobile department store. In 1668, the only year for which we have an itemized record of his wares, he traveled with 17 saddle and pack mules, 13 horses, and three Apache servants. By the time he left Arizona that year, the only merchandise that remained were six pairs of ordinary socks, five pairs of "fine stockings," eight pairs of "fine socks," two pairs of "ordinary gloves," and a pillow covered with embroidered cloth. In trading with Indians, he had acquired 90 deerskins, two of them painted. He also possessed a tent of fine buckskins. To protect himself while traveling, he carried a sword, a harquebus, a knife, a powder belt, and a small axe.

Apparently, Gruber liked to dress nattily. In spite of the dustiness and weariness of the trail, among the settlers he wore a blue cloth coat lined with otter skin and matching trousers.

These were troublous times in what is now the American Southwest. In 1666, crops failed, and a terrible famine began that continued through 1667, 1668, and into 1669. The Indians suffered the most; so many died that the corpses lay unburied along the road, in the arroyos, or at home. In one village alone, more than 450 died of hunger in a single year. Even Spanish colonists had no money to buy corn or wheat from merchants farther south. They grew so hungry, they roasted leather and ate it, until even that was gone.

Meanwhile, Apaches were killing Indians and non-Indians alike, turning the entire region into a war zone. "No road is

**ON THE ROAD INTO NEW MEXICO,
A SETTLER REPAIRS HIS WAGON WHEEL.**

safe," wrote Fray Juan Bernal, the Inquisition's representative in New Mexico. "Everyone travels at risk of his life." The Apaches hurled themselves at danger "like people who know no God nor that there is any hell."

At first, in all this chaos, Gruber continued to do well. He had long since made his own private peace with the Apaches, and they left him alone. He had plenty of money to buy food. In the fall of 1666, he loaded his merchandise onto his mules and set out from Sonora as usual. He traveled through Apache territory and traded with them. By December, he had reached the mission at the Indian village at Quarai, in central New Mexico.

In some ways, Quarai was incredibly remote — two or

three days' journey on horseback from Santa Fe, a day's hard ride from the Río Grande. But the population reflected an ethnic diversity. In addition to the native peoples, known as Humanas, there were Spanish settlers and friars. A popular local politician, Capt. José Nieto, was half black and half Spanish. Nieto's wife, doña Lucía López de Gracia, was part Spanish and part Indian. Nieto's adopted son, 10, and the boy's uncle, both named Francisco, were reportedly half Indian and half Chinese.

On Christmas morning, Captain Nieto, who was the *alcalde mayor* (mayor and judge) of the Salinas region, went to early Mass. So did Gruber and the two Franciscos, who sat together in the choir. As the priest intoned the gospel, Gruber showed the two Franciscos slips of paper on which he had written some letters.

Whispering loudly enough so that others sitting nearby overheard, Gruber said, "In my country, they say that if you chew one of these papers and swallow it while the priest is saying Mass on Christmas day, it will make you completely invincible to any sword or bullet for 24 hours."

The boy and his uncle stared at the papers, on which Gruber had written, +A.B.V.A.+A.D.A.V.+

The older Francisco took a paper and ate it.

After church, the boy and his uncle wandered into the kiva. Some Indians were already there. The older Francisco astonished them by pricking himself repeatedly with an awl. "It doesn't hurt," he said.

From there the two Franciscos went to find doña Lucía and her friend, Madalena Montaño. This time, the older Francisco cut himself with a dagger, then a knife. Again, he said it didn't hurt.

When another relative, named Juan, heard what was happening, he went to find Gruber. But instead of scolding the German, Juan asked for one of the papers. Gruber gave it to him, and he ate it.

To see what would happen next, Juan cut himself with the dagger in doña Lucía's presence.

He said he felt nothing, but she snatched the dagger away from him.

Presumably, doña Lucía took the awl and the knife away, too, and that ended the experiments with Gruber's "charmed" pieces of paper.

But it didn't end the discussion. She told her husband, Captain Nieto, what had happened, and a few days later the two reported the incident to a friar. He sent for Juan Martín Serrano, who had been sitting in the choir near Gruber and the two Franciscos.

"Do you know or understand this writing?" the friar asked them.

"Yes," Juan Martín said. "I saw it on the papers Bernardo de Uber had." Gruber had also gone to Juan Martín's house, where he had written the letters on a wall. The German had promised to return on a certain day and write the words on paper, but he hadn't.

Another witness confirmed what the others said, except that he believed Gruber had written "+A.B.N.A.+A.D.N.A.+" He also said that Gruber had marked 11 pieces of paper.

The friar called Gruber in. "You're a bad Christian," he told the German.

Gruber sulked at the scolding and resumed his traveling sales. At Isleta, the unrepentant German showed similar papers to a Spaniard, Capt. Cristóbal de Holguín. "In Germany, we eat these papers when we go to war," Gruber said. "So if you eat this, you'll be safe from Apache arrows and from bullets and swords."

In spite of the warnings Gruber had received from the Jesuit in Sonora and the friar in Quarai, he clearly didn't consider himself to be in any kind of danger from religious authorities.

In fact, when Gruber reached Santo Domingo, he complained to the head friar that the friar in Quarai had called him a bad Christian and "other similar names." The Santo Domingo friar asked Gruber what had led him to write the words in the first place.

"I wanted to make myself invulnerable," the German replied.

"Where did you see these words?"

"In a little book."

The friar asked to see the book.

"I don't have it. I saw it in Germany."

This friar scolded him, but presumably, as far as Gruber knew, that ended the matter. He sold his remaining merchandise and returned to Sonora in the spring of 1667.

Meanwhile, in New Mexico, the friars talked among themselves. They interviewed the Nietos and other witnesses. It was clear to them that Gruber had committed heresy, and they ordered Captain Nieto to arrest him next time he appeared.

The following spring, when the wandering merchant returned, Nieto arrested him and confiscated his horses, mules, and other possessions. Nieto's men also carried off Gruber's servants. Although well armed, Gruber didn't resist. They took him to the nearby mission of Abó and put him in chains. From there he was moved to the Sandía area, to the hacienda of Capt. Francisco de Ortega, who kept him prisoner in a secure room, watched over by a guard.

Nieto turned Gruber's possessions over to the *alcalde mayor* of the Isleta district, who agreed to keep them safe, but warned that Apaches might steal the horses. The alcalde also kept a list of customers who owed Gruber money, a total of 92 pesos.

The law required the local agent of the Inquisition to investigate the charges thoroughly, then send the defendant to Mexico City to stand trial. But between the famine and the uproar about the Apaches, Gruber remained imprisoned at the hacienda in Sandía for the next 12 months. During that time, he filed a complaint, asking that Captain Nieto return 41 mules and horses taken from him.

Meanwhile, Fray Juan Bernal, the Inquisition's agent, reinterviewed everyone he could find related to the case, including the Nietos. Although Bernal seems not to have doubted Gruber's guilt, he wanted to do as thorough a job as possible.

He fretted that he couldn't interview Madalena Montaño or her husband. She was dead, and her husband lay dying of fever in a remote area too dangerous to visit, because of the Apaches.

In April 1669, Fray Juan wrote to the Holy Tribunal in Mexico City stating that because of the famine and the war with the Apaches, it wouldn't be safe to send Gruber to Mexico City until the triennial caravan of wagons went south in November. Even then, Fray Juan said, he could send Gruber south only if the Holy Tribunal first sent up supplies with which to buy food to feed Gruber on the trip.

When November came, the wagons went south without Gruber. Another half year passed.

At some point, the imprisoned German must have despaired of ever being free again. He knew the consequences could be serious, but Gruber arranged with an Indian named Atanasio, who may have been one of his former Apache servants, to help him escape. Atanasio procured five horses, two saddles, and a harquebus. On the night of June 22, 1670, the Indian appeared with the horses and gun outside the window of the room where Gruber was imprisoned. The two men broke the bar out of the window, then fled southward, down the Río Grande.

His jailer notified the authorities, and a party of eight soldiers and 40 Christian Indians set out after the fugitives, with orders to pursue them all the way to El Paso. Gruber was reported to be wearing his blue cloth coat, lined with otter skin, and the matching pair of pants.

The soldiers searched and searched, but Werner Gruber and his rescuer had vanished.

Five weeks later, on Wednesday, July 30, an officer named Francisco del Castillo Betancur was traveling with four other soldiers on the road that connected Nuevo México with Parral, Nueva Vizcaya (Chihuahua). Between Las Peñuelas and El Perrillo, one of the soldiers, Capt. Andrés de Peralta, went off a little ways from the road. The others heard him shouting and followed.

Tied to a tree by a halter lay a dead horse, still well enough preserved to be identified as roan colored.

Nearby, the soldiers found a blue coat, lined with otter skin, a matching pair of pants and some other, much-decayed pieces of clothing.

Although the soldiers hadn't been searching for Gruber, they had heard of his escape, and they recognized the blue coat and trousers as his.

Searching further, the soldiers found hair and more clothing in the brush. Then bones, widely scattered: here a skull, there a rib, then another rib, and another. Animals had left their teeth marks on some bones.

There was no doubt about it, the soldiers decided. These were Gruber's clothes, his hair, his bones.

Of Atanasio, they could find no trace, so the soldiers concluded that the Indian had killed Gruber. Apparently the two had stopped to rest and tied their horses to the trees. Then Atanasio had killed Gruber and fled, leaving the horse tied up, to die a slow death from thirst.

The most obvious flaw in this theory was that horses were extremely valuable, especially among the Indians. If Atanasio — or anyone else — had killed Gruber, the murderer surely would not have left the horse behind. It is also a puzzle that wild animals would have devoured Gruber so thoroughly that only a few bare bones remained and yet left the horse untouched. Moreover, it is odd that while Gruber's suit remained intact, the other clothing had decayed.

At the very least, if the remains did belong to Gruber, the two fugitives must have separated earlier. Conceivably, the desperate Gruber, alone, perhaps delusional with hunger and thirst, could have died at his own hand, trying to prove that the letters on his pieces of paper really worked.

But there's another possibility. Consider the contrast between the bare, scattered human bones and the horse's well preserved remains. And consider the contrast between Gruber's nearly intact suit and those other, badly decayed bits of clothing.

Maybe when Gruber and Atanasio stopped to rest, they found the skull, bones, and decayed clothing of someone else. They decided to leave Gruber's distinctive clothes behind and sacrifice one of the horses so that anyone pursuing them would think Gruber dead. They disappeared safely into Apache country and lived out the remainder of their lives there.

It could have happened that way, but we'll probably never know more than this: In the end, one way or another, Werner Gruber, Bernardo de Uberque, escaped the Inquisition.

Although Gruber had been imprisoned for more than two years, he had not been convicted or even excommunicated. When the report of his death reached Mexico City, the Holy Office decided to honor what it believed to be his remains with a Christian burial. It ordered that the goods Captain Nieto had confiscated from the German merchant should be sold to pay for burial of the bones and an accompanying Mass.

*Que en paz descanse.*
*Ruhe in Frieden.*
May he rest in peace.

CHAPTER ELEVEN

# Magical Realism on the Frontier
## Believe It Or Not, Spanish Colonial Style

*New Spain's frontier (now the American West)
truly was a strange and bizarre place, full of
customs, people, languages, animals, and plants
that existed nowhere else on earth. Partly as a
result, settlers showed a strong tendency toward
the same kind of magical realism that resurfaced
in the 20th century in fiction. Supernatural
tortures and talking snakes were just a few
of the challenging oddities they faced.*

———

EXPLORERS AND COLONISTS STRUGGLED TO DECIDE: COULD these stories that seemed so implausible really be true? As Fray Francisco de Escobar put it, in 1605, "Each one may believe what he wishes."

An early, vivid account of magical realism among Indians comes from the pen of castaway Alvar Núñez Cabeza de Vaca.

While Cabeza de Vaca developed his skills as a healer and medicine man, he and his three fellow refugees stayed for eight months among the Avavares tribe. Again and again, the Avavares told them anxiously about someone they feared very much. They called him simply Mr. Badthing. He wasn't around just at present, but they worried that he might come back.

Mr. Badthing had first appeared about 15 years earlier — some time around 1519. He was a little man, with a bushy beard that completely hid his face. Sometimes when people were performing a sacred dance, he would appear without warning among them, dressed now as a man, now as a woman. He danced in a wild and crazy way.

When people offered Mr. Badthing food, he always refused. Never once did they see him eat.

When they asked Mr. Badthing where he lived, he pointed to a crevice in the earth.

All this would have been terrifying enough, but it was just the beginning.

When Mr. Badthing appeared at their door, people's hair stood on end. Nothing they did could stop him from entering. As Mr. Badthing rushed into a house, a blazing brand would shine at the door. Then he would seize one of the frightened inhabitants and gash him in the side with a razor-sharp flint, two palms long.

Next Mr. Badthing would thrust his hand into the wound, pull out the person's intestines, cut off a piece a few inches long, and throw it on the fire. Then he would make three slashes in a person's arm, the second at the inside of the elbow, before slicing the arm completely off.

Most remarkably, after Mr. Badthing had completed this gruesome torture, he would replace the limb and, with just the touch of his hands, heal every wound.

After terrorizing the Avavares and others for some time, Mr. Badthing disappeared. But the memory of this evil apparition remained so strong that a decade and a half later, the Avavares and others remained terrified.

At first Cabeza de Vaca had as much difficulty believing their gruesome story as we would today. "What proof do you have?" he asked.

His disbelief offended his hosts, but they fetched the proof: tribal members who had scars in their sides and arms corresponding to the story.

Cabeza de Vaca and his companions grew confused. There was only one possible explanation: Mr. Badthing was the Devil himself.

Surprisingly, that thought comforted them. If God had

protected them through everything else they had endured, He would surely protect them from the Devil.

"As long as we are here, you know you are safe," Cabeza de Vaca told people. "Just believe in God and become Christians like us, and Señor Badthing will never dare bother you again."

According to Cabeza de Vaca, these words delighted the Indians, and they stopped being so afraid.

Nearly five decades later, members of the Chamuscado-Rodríguez Expedition, which traveled north in 1581, came to some remarkable conclusions when they observed a Pueblo Indian ritual, the rattlesnake dance.

One Indian sat on an elevated chair at an altar, and people danced around him. Two men carrying rattlesnakes danced among the crowd. The Spaniards thought the snakes were pottery, or wood, until they heard them rattle.

The snakes coiled around the two dancers' necks and crept up and down their bodies. Then the dancers held the snakes out and, falling on their knees, presented them to the seated man. Rattling loudly, the serpents crawled across his body and along his arms. When they arrived at his throat, the man stood up suddenly and swung around, causing the snakes to fall off. They coiled, and the two snake dancers knelt down, put the snakes in their mouths, and left.

But that wasn't all.

Twelve dancers carrying willow whips stood beside the man at the altar. During each part of the ceremony, each man flayed him with the willow whip 36 times. The man bled so much that the Spaniards expected him to collapse, but he gave no indication that he felt any pain.

"On the contrary," wrote Hernán Gallegos, the expedition's chronicler, "he talks to a large snake as thick as an arm, which coils up when it is about to talk."

Each time the whipped man called to the snake, the giant reptile coiled up and answered, Gallegos reported.

Remembering the Biblical story of Adam and Eve in the Garden of Eden, the explorers decided that, once again, the

**OÑATE TRIED SCOUTING A ROUTE
TO THE PACIFIC OCEAN.**

Devil had taken the form of a snake. Moreover, it was clear to them that the Devil had these people enslaved.

If the Spaniards felt any fear in the Devil's presence, Gallegos didn't mention it. Instead, he saw all this as a justification for their own presence among the Indians. "For this reason, God our Lord willed that the settlement and its idolatrous people should be discovered, in order that they might come to the true faith."

Two decades later, in 1604, Fray Francisco Escobar accompanied don Juan de Oñate across what is now Arizona in search of the South Sea — the Pacific Ocean. Crossing northern Arizona, the explorers followed the east bank of the Colorado River downstream.

A little north of the Gila River, Oñate showed Indians some silver buttons, a silver plate, and a silver spoon.

"Have you ever seen metal like that?" he asked.

Yes, said the chief, whose name was Otata. About 80 miles to the west lived people who made large bowls out of this metal. To cook their meat, they set the bowls right over the fire. The metal came from a mountain range on an island. Some people on the island even had metates made from this metal.

Fray Escobar told himself that no matter what the Indians said, the metal surely wasn't silver. It was probably tin.

Otata also said that 80 miles beyond that, some people lived on the shores of a lake and wore gold on their wrists.

The friar wondered — could it really be gold, or was it just brass? "There is no proof that the yellow metal is gold or that the white is silver," Escobar reminded himself in his notes.

Continuing on, the travelers left 20 horses in care of some Indians along the Gila. When they returned, 13 horses had been eaten. The caretakers said no, no, they hadn't eaten the animals, it must have been someone else.

The friar didn't believe them.

California at that time was thought to be an island. When the explorers reached the point where the river they called Good Hope — the Colorado — met the Gulf of California, the explorers believed they were dipping their feet in the open Pacific. But when the Indians told them — correctly — that large pearls could be found, Escobar and the others doubted, because the Indians didn't show them a single pearl.

Heading home, the explorers returned by the same route. When they reached Otata and his tribe again, Escobar asked the Indians once more about their stories of silver and gold. They surprised the friar by telling exactly the same stories they had told before, "without contradicting themselves in any detail, even though more than 40 days had passed since they had furnished us this information." Escobar was beginning to believe.

Then Otata sketched a map of the land to the west. One nation there was called Esmalca Tatanacha, which, as the friar understood it, meant something like Ear Country. The inhabitants' ears were so large and long that they dragged along the ground. In fact, their ears were so large, people used them like awnings: Five or six people with ordinary ears could stand under the ear of a single person in Esmalca Tatanacha.

In a land near Ear Country, an entirely different part of the anatomy grew unbelievably large. Wrote Escobar, "Men had virile members so long that they wound them four times around the waist, and in the act of copulation the man and woman were far apart."

The friar did not attempt to translate the name of this country, which was Medará Quachoquata.

In one country on Otata's map lived people who had only one foot. In another, people slept in trees.

Then Otata said that the people who wore gold bracelets didn't just live on the shores of a lake. They slept underwater at night.

"The monstrosities did not end there," Escobar wrote. In still another nation, people slept standing up, while balancing a burden on their heads. In another, people had no exit to their digestive tract. For this reason, Escobar wrote, they never ate anything, but "sustained themselves solely on the odor of their food."

Finally, Otata's map of California indicated an island where all the men were bald. A woman who was a giant ruled this island. She lived with her sister, and they were the last of their kind.

As Oñate, Escobar, and their fellow travelers crossed Arizona on their way home to the Río Grande, they asked everyone they met if Otata's stories were true. Again and again, the Indians said yes. Some said they had seen such people themselves; others said they had only heard of them.

By the time Escobar reached home, his skepticism had abandoned him. The friar reasoned that since God was able to create such marvels, He may well have done so. "Furthermore, these Indians were not the first inventors of such news, for there are many books which treat of them and of even greater monstrosities, things of great amazement." In other words, if other people could write about, and believe, such things, why couldn't he?

Did Otata and the other Indians that Escobar encountered

believe these tales, as the Avavares believed theirs about Mr. Badthing? Or were they merely having a good time dazzling — and hoodwinking — the credulous strangers with amusing tall tales?

We don't know.

Today, we may smile knowingly at the friar's acceptance of the stories about the people with the awning-sized ears and other remarkable appendages. But there are many tales from New Spain's northern frontier that historians still cannot identify as fiction or fact.

Was it true, as the Jesuit Ignaz Pfefferkorn reported in the 1700s, that some native women near the present-day Arizona-Sonora border had breasts so long that they just flung them over their backs to where their babies rode and nursed them that way?

Was it true, as later writers reported, that Spanish explorers in 1540 found Chinese ships near the mouth of the Colorado and that the Chinese were mining nearby?

Did the Greek sailor Apóstolos Valerianos, who claimed to have discovered the Strait of Anián — the Northwest Passage — in 1592, get anywhere close to the body of water that still bears his Spanish name, Juan de Fuca?

Is there any chance at all that explorers in 1640 did indeed navigate the only true Northwest Passage, the Arctic Ocean, as was later claimed?

Most such stories may have started with some small fragment of fact. Even the Avavares tales of Mr. Badthing may have begun with a straightforward truth, around which a more elaborate story formed. In 1519, about the time of Mr. Badthing's reported appearance, the mapping expedition of Alonso Alvarez de Pineda discovered the Mississippi River. The explorers traveled along the Texas coast, and spent more than 40 days ashore, possibly along the Río Grande. Mr. Badthing and the blaze of light may have been a wandering sailor with a gun.

As to the woman who ruled an island, even today, in

eastern Washington, the story endures among native peoples of a time when the world was a small island ruled by a woman who was a giant.

As Escobar wrote to the viceroy in 1605, "Only at great risk of not being believed do I venture to report these things."

# CHAPTER TWELVE

# Into the Culinary Unknown

## Rats, Powdered Popcorn, and Other Treats

*Soon after Ignaz Pfefferkorn's arrival on the frontier, an Indian hunter approached, wearing a collection of roasted rats and mice across his shoulder and chest like a bandoleer. He unshouldered the animals and offered them to Pfefferkorn for dinner, but the priest shook his head and said, "I'm not used to such delicacies." The hunter left, amazed at what a barbarian this newcomer was.*

———

WHEREVER SPANISH EXPLORERS WENT, FROM TEXAS TO Alaska, from Nebraska to California, they wrote home about the food. The settlers who followed them sometimes had to struggle to adapt to the strange tastes, especially when, like Pfefferkorn, they came to the frontier directly from Europe. Pfefferkorn, a Jesuit priest who came to the New World to live and work among the Indians, endured the new food, but seldom did he like it.

When Pfefferkorn moved to the Pimería Alta — what is now southern Arizona and northern Sonora, Mexico — in 1756, he brought with him a taste for the foods of his native Germany: roasted lark, snipe patties (made from the meat of a bird), porridge made from peas, and pastries.

Over time, his favorite indigenous food became cakes made from local cactus fruit — providing, that is, "that clean hands have made them." Generally, though, the German priest considered what the Indians ate "in part bad, in part insipid and nauseating."

As for the Spanish colonists, Pfefferkorn's culture shock went well beyond the food. The colonists "have a real genius for idleness," Pfefferkorn said. They refused to walk. Instead, they rode their horses from house to house. And like the Spanish colonists of New Mexico, those in the Pimería Alta loved to sit around and smoke. They even smoked when they got up in the night. Children as young as 10 puffed cigarettes and cigars. Pfefferkorn, who visited many colonial homes, reported that it was a great honor for a woman to light a cigarette, touch it to her lips, then hand it to a male guest.

Maybe the colonists were idle, as Pfefferkorn said. But the record suggests that when they weren't smoking, they were gathering and preparing food, an exhausting daily task. Except in emergencies, they didn't eat rats and snakes. Otherwise, the everyday meals of ordinary people closely resembled Indian fare.

The colonists ate corn daily. At harvest time, they stuffed themselves with fresh, tender corn on the cob: *elotes*. They dried the rest right on the cob for use throughout the year.

The simplest way to prepare this dried corn was to boil the cobs in water until the kernels burst, grew soft, and could be removed easily from the cob. Colonists ate "this insipid dish, called *posole*, without further ado," Pfefferkorn wrote.

When the softened kernels separated from the cob, pulp remained. Frugal colonial housewives pressed, strained, ground, and cooked the pulp and served it as a breakfast drink called *atole*. "Its taste is not tempting," Pfefferkorn said. Some colonists did mix chocolate into their *atole*, but as Pfefferkorn put it, "The drink which is thus prepared is pleasing only to one who has been accustomed to it from childhood."

When colonists traveled, they carried *pinole*. To prepare it, cooks soaked corn kernels and allowed them to dry. Then they roasted the corn in an earthenware dish placed over a fire, stirring the kernels continually so they wouldn't burn. As the kernels cooked, they burst open and took on the appearance of snow-white flowers — popcorn. These *esquitas*, as colonists called them, were "not unpleasant to eat," but for the colonists they were simply a step toward *pinole*. Using *mano* and *metate* — stone pestle and mortar — women ground the popped corn, turning it into *pinole*.

When traveling colonists grew hungry, they threw two or three handfuls of this powdered popcorn into a bowl or basket, added water, and drank it down. To make his own *pinole* palatable, Pfefferkorn added cinnamon and sugar.

Even tortillas challenged Pfefferkorn's tastebuds — he considered them "disagreeable and not at all to the taste of the foreigner." But Spanish colonists loved tortillas the way Europeans loved the finest bread, and women spent many hours daily preparing them. One step in the time-consuming chore involved peeling off the skins of corn, one kernel at a time.

Pfefferkorn did like the "longish round patties" the colonists called tamales. "No snipe patty tastes as good to a German as a tamale does to an American," he said. (In his day, "American" meant someone who lived in the Americas.)

Beef, too, was a staple, eaten at least once a day.

Domestic cattle went wild easily, partly because, in Pfefferkorn's words, "they are not properly looked after" and partly because Apaches and other Indians chased them for fun. But the settlers had perfected the art of the roundup. Yelling and shouting, they drove the animals down the mountains toward mounted *vaqueros* (cowboys). Each *vaquero* carried an 8-foot pole with a crescent-shaped steel blade attached to one end. With such a tool, a *vaquero* could sever the hind tendons of an oncoming animal and stop it in its tracks.

All that remained was to dodge the rest of the thundering herd, seize the enraged animal by its tail, throw it to the earth, jump on it, tie its legs together, and cut its throat.

After that, people no doubt took a long cigarette break. Then they butchered the animal, melted and rendered the fat, and prepared the meat. In an era without refrigerators, this involved cutting the meat into strips, salting it, and hanging it in the sun to dry. This dried beef became a staple, served at every mid-day meal. From hides, men made ropes and lariats so strong that the wildest steer couldn't break them.

A few dairy cows lived among the wild herds, and Sonorans milked them daily, first lassoing their hind legs and tying them together to make the animals stand still. Pfefferkorn noticed that housewives didn't use the cream to make butter, and he couldn't figure out why. So one time he tried making some himself.

Since he didn't have a regular wooden butter churn, he sewed up a large goatskin, filled it with milk, and hung it on a rope between two trees. Then he spent the entire day tossing, swinging, and shaking the goatskin container.

That evening, he opened his makeshift churn and found not butter, but cheese. He blamed himself for not separating the milk and cream well enough, but eventually he concluded that the real problem was that fierce heat prevented butter from hardening.

In place of both butter and oil, which was outrageously expensive, colonists used two kinds of beef fat in cooking. The first was straight fat, cut away from the fresh meat. They preserved this by melting it and storing it in bladders, cow intestines, or earthenware pots. The second came from boiling fresh bones in a kettle and skimming off the fat that floated to the top. This tasted much better, Pfefferkorn thought, than plain melted fat.

This non-butter spread could make a colonist's pocketbook bulge. Even a skinny cow yielded 60 pounds of fat and another 60 pounds of tallow, used in making candles and soap. At a time when a live cow fetched only 12 pesos, the tallow and fat from one carcass could bring the enterprising colonist 60 pesos in a nearby mining town.

By the time Pfefferkorn reached the Pimería Alta, the Indians had been interacting with Spaniards for more than 200 years, but they still loathed pork so much that they would go hungry rather than eat it. They did raise chickens, but only so they could sell feathers and eggs to the colonists. Their eating habits had changed, though, in one respect. Even more than rats and snakes, they loved the taste of horse and mule.

Both Indians and colonists ate many desert plants, including *pinole* made from ground mesquite beans and agave root roasted until the flesh became tender and sweet, like fine honey. The first few times Pfefferkorn tried it, he got diarrhea. But he persisted. "One has only to continue eating it boldly and the stomach becomes accustomed to it."

The German never did learn to appreciate the culinary delights of such native favorites as lizards, worms, locusts, or caterpillars, but he did adapt eventually to one of the colonists' favorite foods: the chile pepper.

Cultivating chiles required exhausting work, he wrote. The plants had to be watered every other day — a great inconvenience in a land of such sparse rain. And the high-strung plants would grow only in weed-free fields. But colonists considered the work worth it. They roasted fresh green chiles on hot embers and added salt and vinegar. Sometimes they ate so many that their mouths frothed. They allowed some peppers to ripen to their natural red, brown, or black, then strung them up to dry for later use.

It amused the urbane, highly educated Pfefferkorn that colonists considered it healthy to eat these vile pods, but medical scientists two centuries later proved the colonists right.

In the final, time-consuming ritual of this culinary love affair with chiles, colonists removed the seeds and crushed the peppers with *mano* and *metate*. They passed this pulp through a sieve, cooked some meat, cut it into small pieces, heated "a thick chunk of fat" in a pan, then fried the meat and ground chile in the fat. They ate the resulting sauce every day, especially at the evening meal, and served it on dishes ranging from baked eggs to boiled fish.

"No dish is more agreeable to an American," Pfefferkorn said, "but to a foreigner it is intolerable." Unfortunately, a stranger like him had only two choices, he said: to eat dry bread or burn his tongue and gums.

The first time Pfefferkorn tried this chile sauce, he had been traveling for 15 hours and was starving. One mouthful, and tears gushed from his eyes. "I could not say a word and believed I had hell-fire in my mouth." However, bit by bit — after the same sort of "frequent bold victories" that made his stomach adapt to roasted agave — he learned to like the ubiquitous sauce.

The inventive colonists used chile peppers for more than just food.

At night, bats would fly out of their homes in hollow trees, rock crevices, and fissures in adobe walls. The creatures filled the air and swarmed into any house where a candle or lantern burned. There they would roost, stinking up the home as they dropped their caustic urine and guano. They multiplied rapidly, but the colonists found a way to eradicate them. After sealing the windows in his house, a colonist built a fire and let it burn down to coals. Then he threw chile peppers on the embers, hurried out, and shut the door. The fumes killed every bat.

Over time, Pfefferkorn changed his views about native food. Years after the day the Indian man brought him roasted rats, Pfefferkorn pointed out to his readers that it was common for people who ate such foods to live to be 100, still vigorous and healthy. He concluded, "The main reason for this longevity seems to me to be the continual use of simple and natural nourishment."

# CHAPTER THIRTEEN

# A Schooner Vanishes

## Roiling Ocean and Indians
## Thwart Alaskan Venture

*One spring afternoon, 112 sailors and officers
stood in the church of San Blas, Nayarit,
Mexico, south of present-day Mazatlán, and
heard a Mass on their behalf. As they left the
church, they carried an image of the Virgin Mary
and chanted prayers. Then they embarked on a
mission to head 5,000 miles north, all the way
to the 65th parallel, about the site of
present-day Nome, Alaska.*

FOR ALMOST TWO CENTURIES, SUCCESSIVE SPANISH KINGS discouraged exploration along the west coast of North America. If anyone, even Spanish explorers, found the legendary Strait of Anián, linking the north Atlantic and the north Pacific oceans, it would be impossible to keep foreign ships out of Spanish waters.

By 1775, when the Spaniards sailed toward Alaska, the threat of such a discovery seemed imminent. Russian ships had reached Alaska in 1741, and the English Parliament had offered to pay a fortune — 20,000 pounds — to the explorer who discovered the Strait of Anián. Carlos III, king of Spain, decided it was time to firm up Spain's long-standing claims to North America's west coast.

So on March 16, 1775, two ships set sail — the *Santiago*, a massive 225-ton, three-masted frigate, and the *Sonora*, a tiny, 36-foot schooner.

The viceroy of New Spain had given the captains of the *Santiago* and the *Sonora* clear orders. They were to go directly to the 65th parallel — farther north than the Russians had sailed — then follow the coast southward. Where they could, they were to land, plant crosses along the beach, and bury beneath them sealed bottles containing the formal acts of possession in the name of King Carlos III. If they saw foreigners, they were to avoid them. If they saw Indians, they were to treat them well and to attack only in self-defense. On the way home, they were to stop and explore San Francisco Harbor.

Spain's honor was at stake. So was its political and economic power. The situation gave the Mass and the prayers special meaning. But, as if to test the sailors' faith, the first problem developed with San Blas still in sight.

A third ship, the *San Carlos*, sailed with the other two to deliver supplies to soldiers and friars at Monterey, California.

But while still in the harbor, its captain came unhinged. He armed himself with six loaded pistols and threatened to kill a sailor. He called the captains of the *Sonora* and *Santiago* to a council of war. He hallucinated. Finally, the other officers convinced him to go ashore and get medical help.

The incident jangled nerves aboard all three ships and required shuffling of duties. The commander of the *Sonora* was reassigned to the *San Carlos*. Juan Francisco de la Bodega y Quadra, a native of Lima, Peru, took charge of the *Sonora* and its 19 seamen. He was only 32. Bruno de Hezeta, an unseasoned captain fresh from Bilbao, Spain, remained in command of the frigate and its 91 men. He was even younger, only 24, but despite his youth and inexperience in the Pacific, Hezeta was the senior officer, in command of the expedition.

Crises bloomed aboard the frigate. The fore-topmast needed repair. In the first eight days of the trip, the men guzzled 52 barrels of water; by March 31, only 94 barrels remained. Livestock aboard ship began dying from hunger and thirst. When the frigate outpaced the schooner, Hezeta decided to tow the smaller ship. Swirling currents caused the two ships to collide, but with no serious damage. Two days later, a crewman repairing the frigate's damaged bowsprit fell into the water. Currents pushed the two ships not north, but south.

Hezeta grew so busy that from April 3 to May 21, he stopped writing in the journal his orders required him to keep.

Meanwhile, aboard the schooner, life was even grimmer. Ten of Bodega's 14 sailors were *vaqueros* — cowboys who had never been to sea. Quarters were so cramped that the men had to sleep sitting up. There was not even room to walk on the deck.

By May 21, chronic dehydration had weakened sailors on both ships. Two men had begun bleeding at their gums and showing other signs of a sailor's worst enemy: scurvy.

Some relief came on June 9, when the expedition found a harbor along the northern California coast and named it Trinidad, for the Holy Trinity. The crews anchored the ships and went ashore. On a hillside by the beach, they erected a cross, built a makeshift chapel, and took possession of the land in the name of the king of Spain. They filled water barrels, chopped firewood, and loaded it onto the ships. Bodega cut wood for spars and rearranged the rigging on the *Sonora*, making the small boat speedier, but less safe.

Patiently and persistently, the sailors worked to win the loyalty of Indians they encountered at Trinidad. Bodega taught a chief to repeat, in Spanish, "Long live Carlos III." In turn the chief ordered his people to leave the Spaniards' cross standing and to protect it.

One evening, the sailors set up tables on the beach and prepared a feast of mussels and other foods. The Indians brought their wives and children, and they all sat eating and making jokes in the universal language of pantomime.

The king, the law, the viceroy, and the ships' captains had all ordered sailors to avoid paying any attention to native women that possibly could be construed as sexual advances. The crewmen of the *Santiago* and the *Sonora* obeyed so well that one day an Indian man asked, "with a significant sign," if they were really men.

**THE TWO SHIPS WERE TOSSED
ON VIOLENTLY CHURNING SEAS.**

That night, two apprentice seamen didn't return to the ship, as required. When Hezeta learned that one of them had spent the night in the Indian village, he ordered the sailor flogged with the straps of a gun. The Indians begged Hezeta to have mercy, and he suspended the thrashing.

When the Spaniards left, the Indians told them they would go into mourning and urged the visitors to return soon. The explorers sailed northward, happy in the thought that they could relate well to the Indians.

The pleasantness didn't last very long.

The northwest wind, "king of these seas," as a priest

aboard the *Santiago* put it, churned up the water and created heavy rollers. On July 9, the wind intensified. Bodega raised more sail than the small *Sonora's* construction could tolerate. The main topmast gave way, throwing the schooner on end. Just as it was about to go under, another wave slapped the floundering boat at exactly the necessary angle and righted her.

Two nights later, in violent winds and worse seas, the frigate rolled so wildly that it appeared she would lose her topmast. No one aboard could sleep.

In mid-July, the two ships approached land for the first time since leaving Trinidad Harbor. On July 13, off the coast of present-day Washington, Hezeta fired a cannon to signal Bodega and the *Sonora* to join him. Instead, Bodega took off exploring and discovered an island, which he named Dolores Island (Island of Sorrows), today's Destruction Island.

Hezeta overlooked Bodega's defiance. He had worse things to worry about. More men had developed scurvy. The sailors suffered terribly. Their gums bled and their teeth loosened. Their joints stiffened, and their legs ached. They developed open sores that wouldn't heal. The men grew anemic.

That evening, when Bodega returned from exploring, the two ships anchored near present-day Point Grenville along the Washington coast. In the distance, they could see an Indian village, probably Quinault, near the beach. The ill Spaniards, although cautious, hoped to repeat the happy experience they had at Trinidad Harbor.

Some Indians boarded the schooner and traded otter skins and fish for beads and other standard trade items. That evening the natives returned with more food: onions, whale meat, salmon, and sardines. Bodega responded with presents: handkerchiefs, beads, earrings, and rings.

Early the next morning, the Indians returned with their wives and received additional presents. Leaving the Indians aboard ship, Hezeta took his second-in-command, Juan Pérez, and a priest, a doctor, and 20 armed men and headed for shore in a launch. At the time, the schooner was caught in shoals.

Ashore, the captain worried whether the anchor would hold the frigate in the rough waters. Anxious to return to the ship, he asked the priest to forego the usual Mass. Quickly, Hezeta took possession of the coast in the name of King Carlos III. Before boarding their launch for a return to the frigate, the sailors encountered six young Indian men, who traded salmon and other fish for the ever-popular glass beads. The Indians invited the sailors to share a meal, but Hezeta thanked them and declined, and the sailors returned to the frigate.

By then, the visiting Indians had left. While Hezcta waited for Bodega to arrive for a previously arranged meeting, he wrote about the Indians in his journal. Their gentleness and friendliness impressed him, as did the fact that some were light skinned, others dark. All were plump and well built and had beautiful faces. For clothing, they wore sea otter robes and chamois.

Just after noon, Hezeta heard the *Sonora* fire its guns. He assumed that meant Bodega was still having trouble getting free of the sand bank. So he sent his launch over with a cable to help pull them free.

A couple of hours later, Bodega arrived, and he had bad news for Hezeta.

While trapped in the shallows, Bodega had decided to replenish his water supplies. So he armed seven men with cutlasses, pistols, and muskets, and sent them ashore in his only launch, probably at a point just south of the Quinault River. Bodega ordered the men to stay on the beach until the launch returned with him, his pilot, and the empty water barrels.

Through his spyglass, Bodega watched the launch approach shore. The surf was so rough that as the men got out, the boat swamped. Without warning, 300 Indians swarmed out of the thicket and attacked the sailors with knives. The attack came so suddenly that only one man had a chance to draw a gun, and it misfired.

While Bodega watched helplessly, the Indians hacked five of his men to pieces. Bodega ordered the ship's cannons fired, but the *Sonora* was too far from shore, and the shots fell short. Only two sailors escaped the Indians' knives by swimming out into the water.

The Indians ignored them and set to splintering the launch and ripping nails and other bits of iron from it.

Lacking any good way to rescue the swimmers, the desperate Bodega put a barrel over the side of the ship. One of his men paddled it awkwardly toward the swimmers.

Before he could reach them, the swimmers inexplicably swam back toward shore. As Bodega watched through his glass, they disappeared. He couldn't tell if they had drowned or made it to shore.

A flotilla of canoes approached the schooner. As if nothing had happened, the Indians held up their finest hides and offered to trade. The tide was rising finally, and Bodega wanted to clear the sand bank while he could. He pretended to ignore his visitors but prepared, as best he could, for battle, while he maneuvered the schooner. Of his remaining crew, five sat slumped in their cramped beds, too ill with scurvy to move. One sailor took the wheel. One took soundings. One watched from the topmast, searching for shallows. One made cartridges. That left only Bodega and two others free to fight if the Indians attacked.

As the schooner cleared the shallows and headed into deeper waters, the canoes stayed with it. The Indians waited until they thought Hezeta and his men had left the prow unattended. Then those in the lead canoe started boarding the Spanish ship. Even the viceroy would have fired, Bodega decided. He and his men blasted the Indians with a swivel gun and muskets. Six or seven fell dead. Others were wounded. The Indians retreated in their canoes.

These were the first white people the Indians had ever seen, and until that moment, they had known nothing of the power of the strangers' weapons.

When Bodega finished his tale, Hezeta received conflicting advice on whether to attack the Indians or sail away.

Bodega and his pilot wanted to land and punish the

Indians. But Hezeta's second-in-command and other officers urged against such action. The viceroy's instructions were clear. The explorers could attack Indians only in self-defense, and punishment didn't qualify. In addition, the Indians knew the terrain and would be at an advantage; rather than punishing them, the sailors could well be defeated, even killed.

Hezeta decided that if he lost any more men in battle he would have to quit the mission and head back to New Spain. So, he sent a few of his healthiest men back with Bodega to replace those who had died, and the two ships sailed out to sea to continue the mission.

On July 19, Pérez presented Hezeta with a written petition to turn back. Given the contrary winds, it would take another month to reach even a latitude of 50 degrees, the former captain said. But his experiences in these waters the year before told him that it was already too late in the season, and the men were too exhausted and ill. If they didn't turn back now, they risked not making it to New Spain.

Hezeta rejected the petition and pushed on, following the zigzagging course the winds required in order to travel northward.

Five days later, his officers presented him with a second petition, which all of them had signed, repeating Pérez's request.

Hezeta continued on.

The smaller *Sonora* had an even more difficult time with the weather and waves than the *Santiago*. Repeatedly, Hezeta held back his frigate to keep the schooner in sight. But at 10 o'clock on the evening of July 29, in a strong gale, the schooner vanished.

At dawn, Hezeta searched the waters, but could find no ship, no debris. He called a meeting of his officers to ask their advice. Once again they urged him to turn homeward.

Hezeta refused.

The days passed, and the schooner didn't appear. Was it ahead? Was it behind? Had the sea swallowed it? Had Bodega disappeared deliberately? There was no way to know.

Hezeta set course for due north, straight toward land, hoping to encounter the schooner there. For days, the ship sailed through rain and strong winds toward a dark, obscure horizon.

On August 10, the winds died, the sky cleared, and land came into sight. Hezeta determined that he was just south of the 51st parallel. High peaks, heavy with snow, rose in the interior. But the *Sonora* wasn't there.

On August 11, Hezeta's third-in-command, don Cristóbal Revilla, brought the captain a third petition. "We are well aware of your great efforts and anxiety to comply with the orders of his Excellency the Viceroy to reach the 65th degree of latitude," it began. However, the sailors were so sick and scurvy-ridden that they could hardly muster three men to serve a watch. "On one of the extremely critical days that occur often at sea, the ship and its crew will, as we all know, be exposed to the danger of perishing."

When Hezeta asked Pérez's advice, the old pilot replied, "I said the same thing to you a month ago." The rain squalls would continue, and grow worse, he warned.

Hezeta felt torn, but he believed Pérez now. Moreover, the ill had begun to die. Help, in the form of the nearest Spanish outpost, lay over 1,000 miles away, in Monterey.

That day, the *Santiago* turned southward and traveled down the coast. Although the young captain didn't realize it, he was following the west coast of what was to become known as Vancouver Island.

A few days later, four canoes of Nootka Indians approached the ship and bartered sea otter pelts with the sailors. Hezeta marveled at how well the Indians maneuvered the frail, lightweight canoes, but he didn't trust these people. To him they looked exactly like those who had attacked his men. They even dressed the same. And they seemed deceptive as traders. After haggling, they took the Spanish goods but refused to give the agreed-upon pelts in return.

Hezeta pointed his musket at them, and immediately they

turned over the pelts. Their response made the captain think that news of Spanish weapons must have traveled to these Indians.

Meanwhile, as the days passed, hope of reconnecting with the *Sonora* died. The little schooner had vanished.

Hezeta continued southward. For the past two centuries, the rumor had circulated that a Greek pilot known as Juan de Fuca — perhaps the same Juan Griego ("Juan the Greek") whom Drake had kidnapped off the coast of South America — had discovered a strait at about this point. But the weather was dismal enough, and Hezeta was just far enough out to sea, that he missed the strait that did indeed lie where Juan de Fuca claimed. Hezeta concluded that Juan de Fuca was lying.

On the afternoon of August 15, a little south of the 48th parallel, a canoe of 10 Indians arrived alongside the frigate, offering to barter dried sardines and pelts. The crewmen thought they recognized two of the Indians as Quinaults who had come aboard on July 14 — accomplices to those who had killed Bodega's men.

Hezeta decided to capture the two and hold them as hostages to exchange for the swimmers, if they had survived. He invited the Indians aboard, but they declined, so he allowed the trading to proceed.

When the Indians weren't looking, Hezeta had his men drop the grappling iron from the launch onto the canoe.

The iron weighed six *arrobas* —150 pounds — and the men dropped it from a height of 18 feet. But to Hezeta's astonishment, an Indian deflected the heavy iron and hurled it into the water, out of harm's way.

Next, Hezeta ordered his men to fire muskets over the Indians' heads. He hoped to frighten them toward shore, since he believed he could overtake them. But the Indians realized that wind powered the frigate. They paddled into the wind, and Hezeta couldn't reach them. At sunset, he lost sight of the Indian canoe.

The frigate continued southward. As it traveled between two capes, the water seethed, and the currents swirled so swiftly toward the northern cape that even with the sails fully unfurled and the winds in his favor, Hezeta could hardly get clear. He concluded that he was passing "the mouth of some great river or some passage to another sea." He was right. The *Santiago* had arrived at the mouth of the mighty Columbia River.

Hezeta longed to enter the channel and anchor, but his lieutenants told him that with so many men ill, there were not enough to raise the anchor.

Hezeta contented himself with mapping the estuary. Believing it to be a bay, he named it Bahía de la Asunción de Nuestra Señora (Bay of the Assumption of Our Lady).

Juan Pérez and the other men must have watched gratefully when their youthful captain resumed the voyage south.

By the time the frigate reached California waters, 45 sailors were seriously ill, and the remainder suffered some symptoms of scurvy. Although Hezeta had hoped to explore San Francisco Bay, he heeded advice of his officers and continued onward toward Monterey.

At 4 o'clock on the afternoon of August 29, the *Santiago* anchored in Monterey Bay. The next day Hezeta made arrangements at the presidio for care of the 35 most seriously ill men. The launch, open and unprotected from the weather, carried them to shore. One sailor was so ill that when the wind hit his face, he died in the launch. He was buried in the chapel of the presidio.

With the presidio overflowing with sick sailors, the less seriously ill went to the nearby mission of San Carlos Borromeo. There Fray Junipero Serra and his fellow friars nursed them.

Organizing a contingent, Hezeta headed back up to San Francisco Bay to map and explore the port. When he finished, Hezeta returned to Monterey, where his crewmen were gradually recovering.

In all this time, there had been no sign of the *Sonora*. But on October 7, the missing schooner sailed at last into Monterey Bay.

Bodega explained that back on that night in July he had

lost sight of the *Santiago* in the gale. He had searched and couldn't find it. Then he raced northward.

At the 57th parallel, the schooner encountered a tribe of black Indians, who lacked bows and arrows, but used spears. Bodega allowed them to approach the ship only one canoe at a time. Although he announced to the air that all the land he was seeing belonged to King Carlos III of Spain, he did not dare go ashore to make the formal act of possession.

Finally, at the 58th parallel, with his sailors "in a lamentable state and in rags," Bodega turned his tiny ship around and headed back down the coast. Russian explorers had seen some parts of this coast, but he was the first Spanish explorer to arrive this far north. He turned back at about the site of today's Glacier Bay National Park in Alaska.

At the 55th parallel, with no Indians in sight, the men went ashore for water, wood, and the acts of possession. A nearby volcano erupted several times a day. It warmed the air and gave the sailors a break from the miserable cold.

Heading south again, the men fell so sick they couldn't handle the ship, and it nearly capsized in a storm. Even Bodega and his pilot grew too sick from scurvy to function.

Still, the *Sonora* made it to Monterey. If Hezeta felt miffed that Bodega had come so much closer to fulfilling their mission than he, he didn't mention it in his journal. He did write that he had to remain longer in Monterey than he had planned to allow Bodega and his men time to convalesce.

On October 25, Pérez, that cautious, veteran sailor who had always put his men's welfare over personal gain or Spanish glory, fell ill with the chills, rashes, and headaches that signaled typhus. However, most of the younger men had recovered by then, and Pérez's illness didn't stop him from sailing with the others on November 1 for San Blas.

At 6 o'clock the next morning, Pérez died. A friar celebrated Mass, and his grieving comrades fired the cannons and a round of musket shots.

When Pérez's wrapped body slid into the sea and disappeared, it became a symbol of what was to happen next. Like the old pilot, Spanish dreams for holding onto the land north of California perished in the coming years.

# CHAPTER FOURTEEN

# A Stranger in a Strange Land

## Mongo Meri Paike in St. Afee

*Spanish colonial laws forbade U.S. citizens (or Anglo-Americans as the Spaniards called them) and other foreigners to enter Spanish territory without permission, which almost was impossible to get. Those without permission were assumed to be spies. In the days after the Louisiana Purchase, officials in New Spain knew that the United States was looking west for more land, so they had reason to eye strange foreigners with unease. The question was not if an invasion would come — but when.*

---

T HE LANDS MAKING UP NEW SPAIN'S NORTHERN FRONTIER were vast, and the number of available Spanish settlers few. Two centuries after the first Spanish colonists settled Santa Fe, it remained the largest community on the entire frontier, with about 4,000 to 5,000 residents.

The city stretched three streets wide and ran for about a mile along the banks of a small creek that fed into the Río del Norte, the river we now call the Río Grande. The plaza lay at the heart of the town. On the north side sat *el palacio*, the old adobe Palace of the Governors, laid out in 1610 by Governor Pedro de Peralta.

Inside that palace one chilly day in February 1807, New Mexico's ailing governor, Joaquín del Real Alencaster, received an unexpected visitor from the tiny settlement of Ojo Caliente, a hard day's ride north of Santa Fe. A few days earlier, two Ute Indians had shown up at Ojo Caliente with the wild-looking white man in tow, saying they had found him alone and on foot in the snow to the north.

The man had scraggly, uncombed hair and a bushy beard that appeared to have been growing unchecked for many months. He was gaunt, emaciated even, and his skin looked pale and unhealthy. The stranger didn't speak Spanish. In French, their only common language, the man told Governor Real Alencaster that he was a physician, a Dr. Robinson. He said he had traveled from San Luís (St. Louis, Missouri) to collect a debt from a Frenchman who was living in New Mexico.

"Where are your companions?" the governor asked.

"I'm traveling alone," the stranger replied.

Although a few Frenchmen reached Santa Fe, Anglo-Americans were nearly unknown. New Mexico remained so unfamiliar in the United States and its territories that American writers commonly called the capital Saint Afee, a misunderstanding that came from the Spanish abbreviation *Sta. Feé*.

San Luís lay 800 miles away. "Your story doesn't make sense," the governor told Robinson. "I cannot believe that you are traveling alone and on foot."

But the gaunt young man insisted he was telling the governor the truth.

The previous summer, Real Alencaster had sent soldiers north through the land once known as Quivira to the Pawnee settlements of what is now Nebraska. Their mission: to turn back Anglo-American soldiers rumored to be exploring territory claimed by Spain. But the plains were too vast, and the soldiers too few, and they returned home without finding the intruders.

It was hard to believe, but there was always a chance that this hungry-looking man might be attached to an American exploring party.

Real Alencaster examined Robinson's papers and read the report from the officer in charge at Ojo Caliente.

"You say you're a physician," the governor said and pointed to his own swollen belly. "How would you treat this?"

When Robinson replied, he spoke like someone who knew medicine, but none of his suggestions matched what Real Alencaster's own physician had prescribed.

One thing was clear. By his very presence, Robinson was breaking the law. The governor arrested him and assigned him to the quarters in which he confined his own officers when they were under arrest. But he also gave him permission to walk around Santa Fe. He sent messengers to determine if the stranger's story about the debt was true. Then he dispatched two soldiers to ride north and try to determine if Robinson really was traveling alone.

Word soon came that the debt was real, but the Frenchman had no money with which to pay. Real Alencaster provided the American intruder with an allowance, gave him two mules, one to ride and one to pack his possessions on, and sent him under guard to a town farther south that needed a resident physician. Then the governor waited to see what would happen next.

There was no doubt in his mind, or the minds of other Spanish colonial officials in New Spain, that the United States would soon seize all of the northern frontier, from Texas to California. The only question was when and how much land they would take. Just the year before, he himself had urged Nemecio Salcedo, the commander in chief of the Interior Provinces of New Spain, to establish forts along the rivers that fed into the Mississippi. But Spain lacked more than manpower. Urgent political problems in Europe prevented commitment of more than minimum resources to the northern frontier of New Spain.

Was Robinson part of the coming invasion, Real Alencaster wondered?

Meanwhile, the governor's two soldiers, one Spanish and one Indian, searched through what is now southern Colorado. Snow lay one *vara* (about a yard) deep and more. It was hard to imagine that anyone but Indians or seasoned trappers could possibly survive out in this frozen wilderness.

But on Monday, February 16, four days after leaving Santa Fe, the two heard what sounded like a shot, just on the other side of the hill. They crested the hill, and there, about half a mile away, they saw two strangers floundering on foot through the snow. A wounded deer lurched away, leaving a dark trail of blood in the snow.

When the hunters saw the soldiers, they ran. The soldiers pulled their lances and galloped after them.

"Amigos. Americanos," the two shabby-looking men called. The one who appeared to be the leader wore blue trousers, moccasins, a red cap, and an improvised coat made from a blanket. The other wore only mud-spattered leggings, a breech cloth, and a leather coat.

The soldiers eyed the Anglo-Americans' weapons, and the Americans eyed theirs.

Beyond those first two words, the Anglo-Americans understood no Spanish, but the one in the red cap spoke French. The soldiers told them that their friend Robinson had arrived in Santa Fe and was being treated well. The man in the red cap responded by saying he was just getting ready to descend the Red River to Natchitoches, Louisiana.

At that the two soldiers grew silent. The Red River was nowhere close. Were these Anglo-Americans crazy? Or were they spies?

Spotting the trail the men had made in the snow, the soldiers followed it through the woods to a meadow. There, on the banks of a tributary of the Río del Norte, rose an astonishing sight: a fort. A sentry motioned threateningly with his gun.

Given the location and the circumstances, the fort was enormous, and it had clearly been constructed with the idea of holding off a heavy attack. Its walls, made of cottonwood logs two feet in diameter, stretched 36 feet across the landscape on each side and towered 12 feet high. Smaller logs that had been sharpened to dagger-like points rose another 30 inches above

**COLORADO'S TOWERING PIKES PEAK
IS NAMED FOR ZEBULON PIKE.**

that, to prevent anyone from scaling the walls. But that wasn't all. Around the perimeter stretched a moat four feet wide, filled with water that the strangers had diverted from the river. They had piled the dirt from the moat against the lower walls, making them impervious to bullets. Over the fort, the starred flag of the United States flapped in the blue Spanish sky.

Two days later, the soldiers galloped into Santa Fe and hurried to the Palace of the Governors. The Anglo-Americans had invited them inside the fort, they told the governor, but there were only a few of them, and they were in pitiful condition. Some had been so badly frostbitten, they could do no work and could walk only with difficulty, supporting their weight on sticks. Incredibly, they had no horses. The leader's name was Mongo Meri Paike, or some such odd foreign name.

Real Alencaster called in Lt. Ignacio Saltelo and told

him to prepare a party of 100 soldiers to ride north. Lt. Bartolomeo Fernández would be his second-in-command. "If the Americans really want to go to the Red River, tell them we will provide all the necessary horses, mules, supplies, and money and escort them there," the governor said. "But they must come to Santa Fe first. Treat them courteously, but don't give them any choice. I want them all here."

In case there were more Americans than the scouts had seen, he ordered Saltelo to take along 100 extra horses to transport the men and their luggage.

Then the governor called in two trusted Frenchmen. "You two approach them first, as friends," he said. "Tell them I have heard the Utes are preparing to attack them, and I am sending soldiers to protect them."

Armed with lances, pistols, and muskets, the soldiers set out.

On the morning of February 26, they arrived in the snowy woods near the fort. The soldiers hung back, out of sight, while the Frenchmen walked into the clearing in which the fort sat.

Fifty yards out, a sentry halted them and fired a pistol into the air. Musket barrels stuck out of the cracks in the fort's walls, ready to fire.

Then the man with the red cap appeared and spoke to them in good enough French. They told him about the impending Ute attack and about the soldiers that were coming to protect them.

The American leader agreed to meet the officers, and Lieutenant Saltelo relayed his message from the governor. "It will be an eight-day journey from Santa Fe to the Red River," he added.

"What? Is not this the Red River?" the Anglo-American leader asked.

"No, señor. El Río del Norte."

Mongo Meri Paike — Lt. Zebulon Montgomery Pike — always claimed later that he believed until that moment that he was camped along the Red River. But he also admitted that he had built his fort with the idea of withstanding a Spanish attack. When Lieutenant Saltelo told him plainly that his fort sat next to the Río del Norte, he knew he stood unequivocally on Spanish soil.

At once he ordered the flag lowered. Then he invited Lieutenant Saltelo and his soldiers into the fort to eat breakfast. Saltelo was astonished to discover the method of entry: by crawling along a plank that crossed the moat, then sliding on one's belly through a tiny opening beneath the wall. The Americans supplied deer meat, and the Spanish soldiers provided *pinole*, biscuits, and goose meat.

By now, the little party of Anglo-Americans had swelled to 15, and Pike explained to Saltelo that another six remained behind. They had all been traveling without proper clothing, in temperatures below zero. They had cut up their blankets for clothing and slept shivering on the frozen ground. The horses had grown so weak that he had left them and a guard some days back and had walked on, with each man carrying about 70 pounds of arms, ammunition, and tools. Two men had suffered such severe frostbite that their feet were rotting, and they couldn't walk at all. Pike had left them behind and had just now sent someone to go for the horses and bring them into the fort.

It isn't clear how much of this Pike told Saltelo. He surely didn't mention that he had recently threatened to kill one of his soldiers for complaining that it was "more than human nature could bear, to march three days without sustenance, through snows three feet deep, and carry burdens only fit for horses."

Lieutenant Saltelo decided to remain at the fort with 50 soldiers, waiting for the stragglers. He wrote a letter to Real Alencaster and told señor Paike he was sending him south in the company of Fernández and 50 men.

"My orders will not justify my entering Spanish territory," the Anglo-American said.

Saltelo was too polite to point out that in that case, Paike had already violated his orders. He said simply that the governor wanted to speak to him in person about his business on the frontier. Since the governor was not well enough to travel, señor Paike would have to go to him.

Paike argued and accused Saltelo of deceiving him, but on February 28, 1807, the Anglo-Americans set out for Santa Fe with Lieutenant Fernández.

The next evening, they reached Ojo Caliente. The little village consisted of one-story adobe houses built together in such a way that their outer walls formed an enclosure, protecting them from attack. Inside this walled town lived about 500 hispanicized Indians of mixed blood. This time, the villagers were expecting the strangers. They fed them and treated them to a fandango dance

As the Anglo-Americans continued southward, the inhabitants of each village vied for the honor of serving as their hosts. They invited the men in, fed them, and allowed their daughters to dress their wounded feet.

Meanwhile, in Santa Fe, the governor received word that Dr. Robinson had admitted to being part of Pike's party. He called in the Frenchman who owed Robinson money and ordered him to intercept Lieutenant Fernández and the soldiers. He was to pretend to be friends with the Americans and see what he could learn.

The Frenchman found them at San Juan Pueblo. He appeared at Pike's door and said in broken English, "My friend, I am very sorry to see you here. We are all prisoners in this country and can never return. I have been a prisoner for nearly three years and cannot get out."

In French, Pike replied that in that case, the man must have committed some crime and that since he himself hadn't, he wasn't afraid.

The man asked so many questions that Pike demanded to know if he was a spy. Only when Pike threatened to run him through with a saber, did the man confess. Then he took Pike to the priest's house and introduced Pike, inaccurately, as the former governor of Illinois. Pike didn't correct him and later wrote in his journal that he enjoyed the extra attention he received as a result of this false impression.

When the priest at San Juan saw Pike's sextant, he looked astonished, like someone who had never seen one before. So Pike showed him how to use it and explained that the sextant allowed travelers to determine their exact location, by measuring latitude and longitude. Pike couldn't understand how such an educated man could be so ignorant of such a basic tool, until the priest told him that the Spanish government still maintained its ancient policy of keeping people in ignorance about geography and similar subjects.

At dusk on March 3, Pike and his soldiers and their escorts reached Santa Fe.

"Its appearance from a distance, struck my mind with the same effect as a fleet of the flat bottomed boats, which are seen in the spring and fall seasons, descending the Ohio River," Pike wrote. The steeples of the two churches gave "a striking contrast to the miserable appearance of the houses."

Santa Feans ran into the narrow streets to see the visitors as the soldiers led them to the Palace of the Governors.

Inside, the men marveled at the buffalo skins, bear skins, and other hides that covered the floors.

Then Governor Real Alencaster arrived to interview these new interlopers on Spanish land.

The conversation took place in French. "You come to reconnoiter our country, do you?" the governor asked.

"I marched to reconnoiter our own," Pike replied.

The governor chose not to comment. If this scraggly looking man in the red hat had actually been on the Red River as he claimed to believe, he would still have been exploring in land that had belonged to Spain for three centuries. But following the Louisiana Purchase, the United States claimed it, and boundary negotiations were even now underway.

"This Robinson, is he attached to your party?" the governor asked.

"No," Pike insisted.

The governor did not reveal that he knew Pike was lying. "How many men have you?" Real Alencaster asked.

"Fifteen."

"And this Robinson makes 16."

"I have already told your Excellency that he does not belong to my party, and shall answer no more interrogatories on that subject."

The governor grew silent. Clearly this man must be a spy. Probably Robinson, too. Why else would they both have lied?

Real Alencaster terminated the interview and asked Pike to return with his papers that evening. He ordered Lieutenant Fernández to take Pike into his own home as a guest and asked the lieutenant and others to watch the American's activities.

When Pike arrived at the Palace again, he brought a small trunk full of papers. "These are my orders," the Anglo-American said, reading them aloud in French. Dated June 24 of the previous year, they stated that Pike was to visit the Comanches, Osage, and other Indians and to invite them to meet with American leaders. That journey could take him up the Arkansas River and back down the Red River to Louisiana, in which case, he was to keep a record of all he saw. He was also to avoid being spotted by the Spaniards, but if he did encounter them, he was to remember that the United States and Spain were on the point of resolving boundary differences. "It is the desire of the President to cultivate the Friendship & Harmonious Intercourse, of all the Nations of the Earth, and particularly our near neighbours the Spaniards," the orders read.

Real Alencaster nodded politely and kept the trunk, so that he and his interpreter could look through the papers for themselves. Then he sent the trunk back and waited.

The next day, Santa Feans plied Pike's men with liquor and questions. Seeing their ragged, primitive clothing, the Santa Feans asked, "Don't you have hats in your country? Do you live there the way the Indians do?"

Pike hovered around, watching as the men got drunker

and drunker. One by one, he pulled them aside and asked them for papers he had given them earlier for safekeeping. Then he hurried back to Lieutenant Fernandez's home and put the papers in the trunk, thinking it would not be searched again.

At that moment, an officer appeared at Pike's door and said he had come to deliver señor Paike, and the trunk, back to the governor.

Silently, Pike followed and watched as the governor and his interpreter went through the papers again.

It appears that this time, among the lieutenant's papers, the governor found an account of Pike's visit to the Pawnees. In it, Pike described how he tried to convince the Indians to swear allegiance to the United States and abandon their ancient loyalty to Spain.

That document alone told Real Alencaster that he could not simply send Mongo Meri Paike back to the United States. The pot-bellied governor informed the emaciated young American in a kind but firm tone that he and his men would have to go to Chihuahua to be interrogated by Nemecio Salcedo. It would be up to Salcedo to decide their fate.

"If we go to Chihuahua, we must be considered as prisoners of war?" Pike asked.

"By no means," the governor replied. He said he would allow the men to keep their arms and would give Pike a certificate that stated he was being forced to go south against his will.

Pike informed Real Alencaster that he would reply to all this in writing, but Real Alencaster dismissed him and said, "You will dine with me today and march afterward to a village about six miles distant."

Pike retorted that he thought it a much greater infringement for Spanish soldiers to trespass in American territory when they visited the Pawnees the previous summer than for him and his little band of men to come to the Spanish frontier with the intention of traveling down the Red River.

Real Alencaster replied politely, "I do not understand you," and dismissed him.

The governor's secretary gave Pike $21 to be used to pay the expenses of his party on the way to Chihuahua. The secretary also handed Pike a new shirt and said it was a present from the governor. His sister in Spain had made the shirt for him, and since he had never worn it, he hoped the Anglo-American would accept it as a gift. Pike, who was still wearing the blue trousers and blanket coat, did.

Now that Real Alencaster had made a decision about what to do with the Americans, he relaxed. At dinner, he plied Pike with fine wine and food from the southern part of New Spain and talked sociably and pleasantly. Afterward, he ordered his coach brought around. It arrived, drawn by six mules and attended by mounted guards. He invited Pike and Lieutenant Fernández to ride the first three miles in the coach with him. At the three-mile mark, he left them with the words, "Remember Real Alencaster, in war or peace."

That very night, one of the Spanish soldiers confided to the American that some people, himself included, wanted Spain to open up the borders and allow trade with the United States. He also told Pike that people were convinced the United States would invade New Mexico the following spring.

On March 5, in heavy snow, the Americans set out on the long ride to Chihuahua, accompanied by 60 soldiers.

Many adventures later, Robinson, Pike, and the others arrived safely back in the United States, and Nemecio Salcedo received a reprimand from the king of Spain himself for permitting "those guilty to be freed." To this day, scholars cannot agree about the real purpose of Pike's visit to Spanish territory, but it is likely that Spanish fears were true, and that he, or Robinson, or both, had secret orders to spy. Certainly Pike's journal and other writings did much to educate the U.S. government about the people, culture, and geography of this nearly unknown land.

Meanwhile, Real Alencaster again urged Nemecio Salcedo to build forts on all the rivers that flowed into the Mississippi, before the Americans did. As soon as the winter snows melted, the governor posted soldiers on the northern and eastern frontiers, with orders to turn back any Americans who might try to make their way to Santa Fe. He also gave orders to every able-bodied man to be ready to take up arms. To Nemecio Salcedo he wrote, "The character of the Anglo-American, his pride and ambition, and the exceedingly weak forces on which I can count for defense, all make my vigilance very important."

But the worst of it, he wrote, was that the Spanish colonists liked the Americans. They didn't want to take up arms against them, and they were talking openly, and without displeasure, of the possibility that the United States would simply seize the northern frontier very soon.

In fact, another three decades would pass before that happened. But just three years after Pike's arrival in New Mexico, the people of New Spain began their 11-year struggle to gain independence from the mother country. Before long, people all along the northern frontier stopped saying, "Viva el rey" (Long Live the King). Instead, the rallying cry across New Spain became, "Viva la virgen de guadalupe, y muera el mal gobierno."

Long live the Virgin of Guadalupe, and death to bad government.

Early in 1998, the U.S. Postal Service asked me for photographs of a new building in Española, New Mexico. Designed by local architect Bernabé Romero, the building is an idealized rendering of the first permanent church the Spanish settlers built after the temporary church they put together hastily in the summer of 1598.

I went out to photograph soon after sunrise. The shadows slanted across the vigas and the straw-colored adobe walls. The sun glinted on the bell towers. The blue New Mexico sky gave sharp outline to the uneven adobe.

A few months later, the Postal Service released the stamp, which honors 400 years of Spanish settlement in the Southwest.

On July 11, 1998, the first day of issue, it had been 400 years and one week since don Juan de Oñate and the first authorized Spanish colonists in what now is the American West arrived at San Juan Pueblo, just north of Española. The July heat was scorching, and sweat poured from the faces of the dignitaries who spoke.

The settlers would have recognized that heat. They described the weather in these parts as "eight months of winter and four months of hell."

They would also have recognized the descendants of their Pueblo Indian hosts. Costumed in eagle headdresses and wings, they danced the sacred eagle dance on the dais, in front of an enormous version of the new stamp. The drums pounded. The dancers swooped and whirled. Whatever outsiders might feel about the Spanish era and Spanish interactions with Native Americans, the Indians from San Juan Pueblo and the Spanish had long since made peace with one another.

Long live the memory of these early pioneers, and long live their descendants. Long live the Native Americans across the West who adapted to these invaders, and other invaders, and survived.

Susan Hazen-Hammond
Santa Fe

**Abó:** ah-BOH
**alcalde mayor:** ahl-CAHL-deh mah-YOR
**Alemán:** ah-leh-MAHN
**Alvarez de Pineda:** AHL-va-res deh pee-NEH-dah
**Amaya, Casilda de:** cah-SEEL-dah deh ah-MAH-yah
**Andrés:** ahn-DREHS
**Angeles, Beatriz de los:** beh-ah-TREES deh los AHN-hell-ehs
**Anián:** ah-nee-AHN
**Atanasio:** ah-tah-NAH-see-oh
**Bahia de la Asunción de Nuestra Señora:** bah-HEE-ah deh la
ah-soon-see-OHN deh noo-EHS-trah seh-NYOH-rah
**Bellido, Diego:** dee-EH-goh beh-YEE-doh
**Bodega y Quadra:** boh-DEH-gah ee KWAH-drah
**Cabeza de Vaca, Alvar Núñez:** AHL-vahr NOO-nyehs cah-BEH-sah
deh VAH-kah
**Castañeda:** cahs-tah-NYEH-dah
**Castaño de Sosa:** cahs-TAH-nyoh deh SOH-sah
**Castillo Betancur:** cahs-TEE-yoh beh-tahn-COOR
**Castillo Maldonado:** cahs-TEE-yoh mahl-doh-NAH-doh
**Cerrillos:** ceh-REE-yohs
**Chamuscado-Rodríguez:** chah-moos-CAH-doh roh-DREE-gehs
**Cíbola:** SEE-boh-lah
**Dorantes:** doh-RAHN-tehs
**Draque:** DRAH-keh
**Escalona:** ehs-cah-LOH-nah
**Escobar:** ehs-coh-BAHR
**Española:** ehs-pah-NYOH-lah
**Espejo:** ehs-PEH-hoh
**Eulate:** eh-oo-LAH-teh
**fanegas:** fah-NEH-gahs
**Fernández, Bartolomeo:** bar-toh-loh-MEH-oh fehr-NAHN-dehs
**Flores:** FLOH-rehs
**Gallegos, Hernán:** ehr-NAHN gah-YEH-gohs
**Gutiérrez de Humaña:** goo-tee-EH-rehs deh oo-MAHN-yah
**Hezeta, Bruno de:** BROO-noh deh eh-SEH-tah
**Holguín, Cristóbal de:** crees-TOH-bahl deh ohlg-EEN
**Hozes, Francisca de:** frahn-SEES-cah deh oh-SEHS
**Jaimez:** high-MEHS
**Jaramillo:** har-ah-MEE-yoh
**Jerónimo:** hehr-OH-nee-moh
**Joaquín:** hwa-KEEN
**Jusepe:** hoo-SEH-peh
**la leyenda negra:** lah leh-YEHN-dah NEH-grah
**Las Peñuelas:** lahs peh-nyew-EH-lahs
**leguas:** LEH-gwahs
**Leyva de Bonilla:** LEH-vah deh boh-NEE-yah
**López de Gracia:** LOH-pehs deh GRAH-see-yah
**Lucía:** loo-SEE-yah
**Luís:** loo-EES

**Mariames:** mah-ree-AH-mehs
**Martín Serrano:** mahr-TEEN seh-RRAH-noh
**Montaño, Madalena:** mah-dah-LEH-nah mohn-TAH-nyoh
**Morlete:** mohr-LEH-teh
**Narváez:** nahr-VAH-ehs
**Nieto, José:** hoh-SEH nee-EH-toh
**Niza, Marcos de:** MAHR-cohs deh NEE-sah
**Nueva Andalucía:** noo-EH-vah ahn-dah-loo-SEE-yah
**Nueva Vizcaya:** noo-EH-vah vees-KYE-yah
**Nuevo León:** noo-EH-voh leh-OHN
**Nuevo México:** noo-EH-voh MEH-hee-coh
**Ojo Caliente:** OH-hoh cah-lee-EHN-teh
**Ojo Triste:** OH-hoh TREES-teh
**Oñate:** oh-NYAH-teh
**Ordóñez, Isidro:** ee-SEE-droh ohr-DOH-nyehs
**Oviedo, Lope de:** LOH-peh deh oh-vee-EH-doh
**Padilla:** pah-DEE-yah
**Peralta:** peh-RAHL-tah
**Perea, Esteban de:** ehs-TEH-bahn deh peh-REH-ah
**Pérez de Luxán, Diego:** dee-EH-goh PEH-rehs deh loo-HAHN
**Pérez Granillo:** PEH-rehs grah-NEE-yoh
**Pérez, Melchior:** mehl-CHORE PEH-rehs
**Perrillo:** peh-REE-yoh
**Pfefferkorn, Ignaz:** IG-natz PFEH-fer-corn
**Pimería Alta:** pee-meh-REE-ah AHL-tah
**Quarai:** kwa-RYE
**Quivira:** kee-VEE-rah
**Real Alencaster:** reh-AHL ah-lehn-cahs-TEHR
**Revilla, Cristóbal:** crees-TOH-bahl reh-VEE-yah
**Romero, Bernabé:** behr-nah-BEH roh-MEH-roh
**Salcedo, Nemecio:** neh-MEH-see-oh sahl-SEH-doh
**Saltelo, Ignacio:** eeg-NAH-cee-oh sahl-TEH-loh
**Sánchez Valenciano:** SAHN-chehs vah-lehn-see-AH-noh
**Sangre de Cristo:** SAHN-greh deh CREES-toh
**Serra, Junípero:** hoo-NEE-peh-roh SEH-rrah
**Sotelo Osorio, Felipe:** feh-LEE-peh soh-TEH-lo oh-SOH-ree-oh
**Tiguex:** TEE-gweks or TEE-weks
**Tirado:** tee-RAH-doh
**Uber, Bernardo de:** behr-NAHR-doh deh OO-behr
**Valeriano, Apóstolos:** ah-POHS-toh-los vah-leh-ree-AH-noh
**varas:** VAH-rahs
**Vázquez de Coronado:** VAHS-kehs deh coh-roh-NAH-doh
**Vicente:** vee-SEHN-teh
**Yquaces:** ee-KWAH-sehs
**Ysopete:** ee-soh-PEH-teh
**Zaldívar Mendoza:** sahl-DEE-vahr mehn-DOH-sah
**Zárate Salmerón:** SAH-rah-teh sahl-meh-ROHN

DEDICATION

PAGE 4    *For God, Glory, and Gold*, detail of the mural, *A Military Chronicle of the Peoples of New Mexico*, Douglas B. Weaver. New Mexico National Guard Headquarters, Santa Fe.

Blending years as a professional illustrator and a lifelong interest in North American history, Douglas B. Weaver uses art to bring to life the compelling, diverse American experience. Weaver was commissioned to paint a three-panel wall mural for the New Mexico National Guard's headquarters. *For God, Glory, and Gold* describes New Mexico's Spanish colonial experience from Coronado to don Juan de Oñate; the treks of Spain's clerics and soldiers to the Pueblo Indian Revolt; the Spanish reconquest to the peace restored by don Juan Bautista de Anza.

ABOUT THE ARTIST

PAGE 7    Susan Hazen-Hammond. Photograph by Eduardo Fuss.

CHAPTER TWO

PAGE 25    Coronado (detail), Bill Ahrendt, "In Coronado's Footsteps," *Arizona Highways*, April 1984.

PAGE 29    Coronado's expedition, Ahrendt, *Arizona Highways*, April 1984.

Ohio native Bill Ahrendt moved to Arizona early on. He trained at the Los Angeles Art Center, the Cleveland Institute of Art, and the Munich Academy. Now living in Arizona's Mogollon Rim country, Ahrendt paints and sketches in the styles of the Old Masters.

CHAPTER THREE

PAGE 37    Spanish official (detail), Ahrendt, *Arizona Highways*, April 1984.

CHAPTER FOUR

PAGE 40    Francis Drake. J. Houbraken engraving (Amsterdam circa 1740). Anne S. K. Brown Military Collection, Brown University Library.

CHAPTER FIVE

PAGE 49    Hand with minerals, Ahrendt, *Arizona Highways*, April 1984.

CHAPTER SIX

PAGE 56    View of *La Puerta del Sol*, steel sculpture, Armando Alvarez. Tomé Hill, New Mexico.

PAGE 59    View of *La Puerta del Sol*.

Born in Mexico City to Basque immigrants, Armando Alvarez became a U.S. citizen in 1948 and has lived in New Mexico since 1993. His sculptures and paintings include five monumental sculptures along the Interstate 25 corridor from the U.S.-Mexico border. Of *La Puerta del Sol*, Alvarez says, "The only thoughts that I had during [its] creation were that we came here to this land from all corners of the earth in search of fortune and happiness and that somewhere along the line we managed to forge this great nation of ours that stands for freedom and democracy."

CHAPTER SEVEN

PAGE 68    Indians and soldiers, Ahrendt, *Arizona Highways*, April 1984.

CHAPTER EIGHT

PAGE 76    16th-century buffalo illustration. *History*, Francisco López de Gómara. Rare Book Division, New York Public Library.

For the past five years, Spokane artists Tom and Lea Anne Askman have collaborated on public arts projects, including the *Royal Road.* Their commission to commemorate New Mexico's Camino Real (Royal Highway) shows different eras in the region's development. Six sculptures along a pedestrian mall progress from the Manso Indians to the Spaniards to the buffalo soldiers to a modern-day child.

Albuquerque native Joel T. Ramirez studied art at the University of New Mexico and has developed his artistic career from his hometown. His richly colored oil paintings  portraying New Mexico's Spanish/Indian heritage in the Southwest have been exhibited internationally and featured in television programs. Besides painting commissions for such major companies as Paramount Pictures and Ford Motor Company, Ramirez has painted multiple works for New Mexico's public art program.

American painter Gerald Cassidy was influential in the Santa Fe and Taos artist communities of the early 20th century. In 1922, the Atchison, Topeka & Santa Fe Railway owned the La Fonda hotel and commissioned Gerald Cassidy to paint 10 figures representing the Southwest. Cassidy's original paintings are scattered throughout the hotel's public areas. Under commission for the Works Progress Administration during the Depression, he painted more such large-scale works to enhance civic buildings around the West.

## DAYS OF DESTINY
### Fate Beckons Desperados & Lawmen

Many a newcomer came West intent on molding a future, grabbing life with both hands and building opportunity. Shifty or bold, desperate or noble, given a trusty horse, a gun, and occasional friends, any man might stand a chance. But every chain of events has one single day, perhaps a fleeting moment, when fate first points a decisive finger and the course of history changes. Delve into 20 tales of how real-life desperados and lawmen faced momentous days that changed their lives forever. Look back through time to see if you can spot when destiny dealt the final hand.

Softcover. 144 pages. Black and white illustrations and historical photographs. **#ADAP6 $7.95**

## MANHUNTS & MASSACRES

Clever ambushes, horrific massacres, and dogged pursuits catapult the reader into days of savagery on the Arizona frontier. If life was hard, death came even harder: A bungled robbery leads to murder. Arizona's largest manhunt imprisons two brothers unjustly. Bloodstained cash traps a family's desperate killer. Reading through these 18 accounts, you'll join the posses in hot pursuit across the roughest terrain and outwit the most suspicious of fugitive outlaws. From the vicious to the valiant, each true story will convince you — the good old days were a challenge that few of us could survive!

Softcover. 144 pages. Black and white historical photographs. **#AMMP7 $7.95**

**TO ORDER THESE BOOKS OR TO REQUEST A CATALOG, CONTACT:**
*Arizona Highways*, 2039 West Lewis Avenue, Phoenix, AZ 85009-2893.
Or send a fax to 602-254-4505. Or call toll-free nationwide 1-800-543-5432.
(In the Phoenix area or outside the U.S., call 602-258-1000.)
Visit us at www.arizonahighways.com to order online.

## THEY LEFT THEIR MARK
### Heroes and Rogues of Arizona History

Indians, scouts, and mountain men gallop through 16 true stories of Western adventure. Before Arizona Territory was ever mapped, its rugged terrain and extreme temperatures demanded much of the explorers who reached it. Even as more and more people came to the Southwest, the land remained rugged, harsh. Those whose names are remembered were individualists who left their unique stamp — good or bad — on Arizona's history: Alchesay, the Apache who led his people in war and in peace; swindler James Addison Reavis, who almost made himself a Spanish baron with an Arizona kingdom; and many more.

Softcover. 144 pages. Black and white historical photographs.
#ATMP7 $7.95

## THE LAW OF THE GUN
### By Marshall Trimble

Recounting the colorful lives of gunfighters, lawmen, and outlaws, historian Marshall Trimble examines the mystique of the Old West and how guns played into that fascination. Tools of survival as well as deadly weapons, guns on the frontier came to symbolize the gutsy independence of idealized Western heroes — even when those "heroes" were cold-blooded killers. With the deft storyteller's touch, Trimble recounts the macabre humor of digging up one dead gunslinger to deliver his last shot of whiskey and the intensity of the Arizona Rangers who faced death down a gun barrel every time they pursued a crook.

Softcover. 192 pages. Black and white historical photographs.
#AGNP7 $8.95

## TOMBSTONE CHRONICLES
### Tough Folks, Wild Times

Ed Schieffelin's hunger for the thrill of discovery survived brutal terrain and warring Apaches. When he at last struck silver, thousands flocked to a rough mining camp that became Tombstone. Rubbing shoulders with Clanton, Earp, and Holliday, ordinary people lived in extraordinary times as Tombstone became an oasis of decadence, cosmopolitan culture, and reckless violence. Curly Bill Brocius, a bully with a sense of rhythm, set folks dancing . . . at gunpoint. Reverend Peabody landed some punches for the gospel. Theirs are some of 17 true stories from an Old West where anything could happen — and too often did.

Softcover. 144 pages. Black and white historical photographs.
**#AWTP8 $7.95**

## STALWART WOMEN
### Frontier Stories of Indomitable Spirit
### By Leo W. Banks

Tough enough to walk barefoot through miles of desert. Strong enough to fell a man with a jaw-crunching blow. Wily enough to con the U.S. Army. You've missed the Old West's full excitement until you meet the unique women who plunged into the harsh unknown — mad Mollie Monroe on her quest for revenge, Sarah Bowman and her gigantic strength, Pauline Cushman daring danger behind battle lines as a spy. These are not fiction, but the gripping reality of tough women fighting for a place in the hostile wilderness. They didn't buckle when disaster struck, and disaster struck often. For danger and adventure, read these 15 riveting portraits of gutsy endurance.

Softcover. 144 pages. Black and white historical photographs.
**#AWWP8 $7.95**

**ARIZONA HIGHWAYS BOOKS**

**TO ORDER THESE BOOKS OR TO REQUEST A CATALOG, CONTACT:**
*Arizona Highways*, 2039 West Lewis Avenue, Phoenix, AZ 85009-2893.
Or send a fax to 602-254-4505. Or call toll-free nationwide 1-800-543-5432.
(In the Phoenix area or outside the U.S., call 602-258-1000.)
Visit us at www.arizonahighways.com to order online.